初級英語檢定複試測驗① 詳解

寫作能力測驗詳解

第一部份：單句寫作

第 1～5 題：句子改寫

1. Susan likes to play basketball.
   Mary and John ＿＿＿＿＿＿＿＿＿ ＿＿＿＿＿＿＿.

   重點結構：單數主詞改為複數主詞

   　解　答：<u>Mary and John like to play basketball.</u>

   句型分析：主詞＋動詞＋不定詞＋受詞

   　說　明：原句的主詞 Susan 為第三人稱單數，故動詞用
   　　　　　　likes；然而改成主詞 Mary and John 後，變成
   　　　　　　複數主詞，故動詞用 like。

2. Mrs. Lee goes to the library every day.
   Mrs. Lee ＿＿＿＿＿＿＿＿＿＿＿＿＿＿＿＿ yesterday.

   重點結構：現在式改為過去式

   　解　答：<u>Mrs. Lee went to the library yesterday.</u>

   句型分析：主詞＋動詞＋不定詞＋受詞＋時間副詞

   　說　明：原句的時間點為 every day，故時態用現在式；改
   　　　　　　為 yesterday 後變過去式，動詞 go 也須改成過去
   　　　　　　式 went。

   * library (ˈlaɪˌbrɛrɪ) n. 圖書館

3. Where is the bus stop?

Do you know _____?

　　重點結構：名詞子句的用法

　　解　　答：<u>Do you know where the bus stop is?</u>

　　句型分析：Do you know + where + 主詞 + be 動詞 + 受詞？

　　説　　明：Do you know 後面須接受詞，故問句 Where is
　　　　　　　the bus stop? 須改爲名詞子句的形式，即「疑問
　　　　　　　詞 + 主詞 + 動詞」，故寫成 where the bus stop
　　　　　　　is。本句的句意爲：「你知道公車站在哪裡？」

　　* ***bus stop*** 公車站

4. This is the boy's book.

_____ the boys' books.

　　重點結構：單數名詞改爲複數名詞

　　解　　答：<u>These are the boys' books.</u>

　　句型分析：代名詞 + be 動詞 + 補語

　　説　　明：原句的主詞補語爲 the boy's book，故 be 動詞用
　　　　　　　單數 is；補語改爲複數 the boys' books 後，主詞
　　　　　　　和 be 動詞都須改爲複數。

5. I usually watch TV in the evening.

I _____ right now.

　　重點結構：現在式改爲現在進行式

　　解　　答：<u>I am watching TV right now.</u>

　　句型分析：主詞 + be 動詞 + V-ing + 時間副詞

説　明：時間副詞改爲 right now，表示現在正在進行的動作，故動詞時態須改爲「現在進行式」，即「be 動詞 + V-ing」的形式，主詞爲 I，故 be 動詞用 am。

* **right now** 現在

第 6～10 題：句子合併

6. Dan has a car.

The car is expensive.

Dan ＿＿＿＿＿＿＿＿＿＿＿＿＿＿＿＿＿＿＿＿＿ car.

重點結構：句子的基本結構

解　答：<u>Dan has an expensive car.</u>

句型分析：主詞 + 動詞 + 受詞

説　明：單數可數名詞的冠詞用 a 或 an，母音開頭的單字前，冠詞須用 an，本句 expensive car 須用 an 當冠詞。

* expensive〔ɪkˋspɛnsɪv〕*adj.* 昂貴的

7. The bowl is empty.

The bowl is on the table.

The bowl that ＿＿＿＿＿＿＿＿＿＿＿＿＿＿＿ empty.

重點結構：that 引導形容詞子句

解　答：<u>The bowl that is on the table is empty.</u>

句型分析：主詞 + 形容詞子句 + be 動詞 + 形容詞

説　明：本句的句意爲：「放在桌上的那個碗是空的。」
that 在此爲關係代名詞，代替先行詞 the bowl，引導形容詞子句，在形容詞子句裡做主詞。

* bowl〔bol〕*n.* 碗　　empty〔ˋɛmptɪ〕*adj.* 空的

8. Lucy didn't pass the test.
   She studied hard.
   Lucy ＿＿＿＿＿＿＿＿＿＿ although ＿＿＿＿＿＿＿＿＿.

   重點結構：although 的用法

     解　答：<u>Lucy didn't pass the test although she studied</u>
           <u>hard.</u>

   句型分析：主詞＋否定助動詞＋原形動詞＋受詞＋although＋
           主詞＋動詞＋副詞

     說　明：本句的句意為：「雖然露西很用功，但還是沒有通
           過考試。」although 當從屬連接詞表「雖然」，引
           導副詞子句。

   * pass〔pæs〕v. 通過

9. Anne dried her hair.
   Anne washed her hair.
   After ＿＿＿＿＿＿＿＿＿＿＿＿＿＿＿＿＿＿ it.

   重點結構：after 的用法

     解　答：<u>After Anne washed her hair, she dried it.</u>

   句型分析：After＋主詞＋動詞＋受詞＋,＋主詞＋動詞＋受詞

     說　明：本句的句意為：「安洗完頭髮後，把頭髮吹乾。」
           用 After（在～之後）來引導副詞子句，表示事情
           的先後順序。在 After 之後寫上 Anne washed her
           hair，而主要子句為 Anne dried her hair，為了
           避免重複 her hair，故用代名詞 it 來取代。

   * dry〔draɪ〕v. 使變乾

10. Alex has a new bike.

His parents gave it to him.

Alex's parents _____ bike.

> 重點結構：give 的用法
>
> 解　答：<u>Alex's parents gave him a new bike.</u>
>
> 句型分析：主詞＋give＋間接受詞（人）＋直接受詞（物）
>
> 説　明：本句的句意爲：「艾力克斯的父母給了他一台新的
> 腳踏車。」
>
> give（給）的寫法有兩種：
>
> $$\begin{cases} \text{give } sb. \ sth. \\ \text{give } sth. \text{ to } sb. \end{cases}$$
>
> 這題要用第一種寫法，先寫人（him），再寫物
> （a new bike）。
>
> * bike〔baɪk〕 n. 腳踏車（= bicycle）

第 11～15 題：重組

11. Father _____.

to / me / some milk / buy / told

> 重點結構：tell 的用法
>
> 解　答：<u>Father told me to buy some milk.</u>
>
> 句型分析：主詞＋tell＋受詞＋to V.
>
> 説　明：「tell sb. to V.」表「叫某人去做～」，
> 本句的句意爲：「爸爸叫我去買些牛奶。」

12. Dave _____.

by train / goes / to / usually / work

重點結構：頻率副詞的用法

解　答：Dave usually goes to work by train.

句型分析：主詞＋頻率副詞＋動詞片語＋by＋交通工具

說　明：主詞 Dave 為第三人稱單數，動詞用 goes，而
usually（通常）為頻率副詞，須放在 be 動詞後，
一般動詞前，故須置於 goes 前。本句的句意為：
「戴夫通常搭火車去上班。」

13. I _____.

sour food, / eat the lemon / don't / so / didn't / like / I

重點結構：so 的用法

解　答：I don't like sour food, so I didn't eat the lemon.

句型分析：主詞＋否定助動詞＋原形動詞＋受詞＋,＋so＋主詞
＋否定助動詞＋原形動詞＋受詞

說　明：連接詞 so「所以」和 because「因為」的比較：
$$\begin{cases} 原因＋so＋結果 \\ 結果＋because＋原因 \end{cases}$$
原因是「我不喜歡酸的食物」，結果是「我沒有吃
那顆檸檬」，so 前面放原因，後面放結果。

* sour〔saʊr〕adj. 酸的　lemon〔ˈlɛmən〕n. 檸檬

14. Did _____ Mary?

call / to / remember / you

重點結構：remember 的用法

解　答：<u>Did you remember to call Mary?</u>

句型分析：Did ＋ 主詞 ＋ remember ＋ 不定詞 ＋ 受詞？

説　明：本句的句意爲：「你有記得打電話給瑪麗嗎？」
remember「記得」有兩種寫法：

$$\begin{cases} \text{remember ＋ to V.} & \text{記得去做…【動作未完成】} \\ \text{remember ＋ V-ing} & \text{記得做過…【動作已完成】} \end{cases}$$

* remember〔rɪ'mɛmbɚ〕v. 記得

　call〔kɔl〕v. 打電話給

15. The boy _____ happy.
the prize / was / who / won

重點結構：關係代名詞 who 的用法

解　答：<u>The boy who won the prize was happy.</u>

句型分析：主詞 ＋ 形容詞子句 ＋ be 動詞 ＋ 形容詞

説　明：本句的句意爲：「這個得獎的男孩很高興。」關代
who 引導形容詞子句，修飾先行詞 The boy，後面
再接 was happy。

* win〔wɪn〕v. 贏得【三態變化：win-won-won】

　prize〔praɪz〕n. 獎；獎品

第二部份：段落寫作

題目： Mrs. Lee 責怪小孩吃了蛋糕。請根據以下的圖片寫一篇約
50 字的短文。**注意**：未依提示作答者，將予扣分。

Mrs. Lee bought a piece of cake to enjoy after she
finished her housework. **When** she came back, she found the
plate was empty. She called her two sons and demanded to
know who had eaten it. Each of the boys blamed the other.
Then they began to fight. **Meanwhile**, Mr. Lee sat in the
next room, enjoying the piece of cake.

　　李太太買了一塊蛋糕，要在做完家事之後享用。當她回來的時
候，她發現盤子是空的。她叫她的兩個兒子來，要求要知道是誰把
它吃了。這兩個男孩都責怪對方。然後他們就開始打架。這時候，
李先生正坐在隔壁房間享用那塊蛋糕。

cake〔kek〕*n.* 蛋糕　　　housework〔'haʊs,wɝk〕*n.* 家事
plate〔plet〕*n.* 盤子　　　empty〔'ɛmptɪ〕*adj.* 空的
call〔kɔl〕*v.* 叫；召喚　　demand〔dɪ'mænd〕*v.* 要求
blame〔blem〕*v.* 責怪　　　fight〔faɪt〕*v.* 打架
meanwhile〔'min,hwaɪl〕*adv.* 同時

口説能力測驗詳解

* 請在 15 秒內完成並唸出下列自我介紹的句子,請開始。

My seat number is (複試座位號碼後 5 碼), and my test number is (初試准考證號碼後 5 碼).

I. 複誦

共五題。題目不印在試卷上,由耳機播出,
每題播出兩次,兩次之間大約有一到二秒的
間隔。聽完兩次後,請馬上複誦一次。

1. Don't forget to lock the door. 不要忘記鎖門。

2. Is Jim here today? 吉姆今天在這裡嗎?

3. Will you take the bus or the train to the city?
   你要搭公車還是火車到市區?

4. Let's go. The movie will start soon.
   我們走吧。電影很快就要開始了。

5. Where did you buy this delicious cake?
   這個美味的蛋糕你是在哪裡買的?

【註】 forget〔fɚˋgɛt〕v. 忘記　　lock〔lɑk〕v. 鎖
　　　 delicious〔dɪˋlɪʃəs〕adj. 美味的

II. 朗讀句子與短文

共有五個句子及一篇短文，請先利用一分
鐘的時間閱讀試卷上的句子與短文，然後
在一分鐘內以正常的速度，清楚正確地朗
讀一遍，請開始閱讀。

One : Don't forget to order some food for lunch.

不要忘記點一些食物當午餐。

Two : When did you last go to the movies?

你上次去看電影是什麼時候？

Three : Hand me that dictionary, will you?

把那本字典拿給我，好嗎？

Four : Were you able to find the papers you wanted?

你能夠找到你要的那些文件嗎？

Five : Because he didn't pass the driving test, John didn't
get his license.

因為沒有通過駕駛考試，所以約翰沒有拿到駕照。

【註】 order〔ˋɔrdɚ〕v. 點（餐）　　last〔læst〕adv. 上次
go to the movies 去看電影
hand〔hænd〕v. 交給；拿給
dictionary〔ˋdɪkʃənˏɛrɪ〕n. 字典　　*be able to V.* 能夠…
papers〔ˋpepɚz〕n. pl. 文件　　pass〔pæs〕v. 通過
the driving test 駕駛考試　　license〔ˋlaɪsn̩s〕n. 執照

Six　：If you have to spend a long time on an airplane, wear loose, comfortable clothing. You should also wear layers so that you can take them off or add them if the temperature changes. Stretch your muscles before, during, and after the flight to prevent soreness. Also avoid salty food and drink a lot of water. This will all make your flight more comfortable.

如果你必須在飛機上度過很長的時間，你要穿著寬鬆、舒適的衣物。你也應該穿好幾層衣服，以便於如果溫度改變，你可以脫衣服或添加衣服。在飛行前、中、後，都要伸展一下肌肉，以預防酸痛。也要避免太鹹的食物，並且多喝水。這所有的一切都將使你的飛行更加舒適。

【註】 spend〔 spɛnd 〕 v. 度過　　airplane〔ˈɛr͵plen 〕 n. 飛機
loose〔 lus 〕 adj. 寬鬆的
comfortable〔ˈkʌmfɚtəbl̩ 〕 adj. 舒服的
clothing〔ˈkloðɪŋ 〕 n. 衣服　　layer〔ˈleɚ 〕 n. 層
so that 以便於　　　**take off** 脫掉
add〔 æd 〕 v. 添加　　temperature〔ˈtɛmprətʃɚ 〕 n. 溫度
change〔 tʃendʒ 〕 v. 改變　　stretch〔 strɛtʃ 〕 v. 伸展
muscle〔ˈmʌsl̩ 〕 n. 肌肉　　flight〔 flaɪt 〕 n. 飛行
prevent〔 prɪˈvɛnt 〕 v. 預防　　soreness〔ˈsornɪs 〕 n. 酸痛
avoid〔 əˈvɔɪd 〕 v. 避免　　salty〔ˈsɔltɪ 〕 adj. 鹹的

III. 回答問題

共七題。題目不印在試卷上，由耳機播出，
每題播出兩次，兩次之間大約有一到二秒的
間隔。聽完兩次後，請馬上回答。每題回答
時間爲 15 秒，請在作答時間內儘量地表達。

1. **Q** : How did you get here today?
   你今天是如何到這裡的？

   A1: I came by bus. I took the number 23. It didn't take too long.
   我搭公車來的。我搭 23 號公車。沒有花太久的時間。

   A2: I drove myself. It took me about thirty minutes. The traffic wasn't too bad.
   我自己開車來的。花了我大約 30 分鐘的時間。交通狀況還算不錯。

   【註】 take〔tek〕v. 花費（時間）
   myself〔maɪˈsɛlf〕pron. 我自己
   traffic〔ˈtræfɪk〕n. 交通

2. **Q** : What will you do after this test?
   這個測驗結束後你會做什麼？

   A1: I plan to go straight home. My family is waiting for me. They'll be anxious to hear how I did.
   我打算直接回家。我的家人正在等我。他們會急著想聽到我考得如何。

A2: I'm going to meet a friend nearby. We'll meet at a coffee shop. It's a good chance for us to catch up.

我會在附近和朋友見面。我們會在一家咖啡廳見面。這對我們來說是一個可以聊聊近況的好機會。

【註】 straight〔stret〕adv. 直接地
anxious〔'æŋkʃəs〕adj. 渴望的　　do〔du〕v. 表現
meet〔mit〕v. 與…見面　　*coffee shop* 咖啡廳
nearby〔'nɪr'baɪ〕adv. 在附近
chance〔tʃæns〕n. 機會　　*catch up* 聊近況

3. **Q** : What is important to you, love or money? Why?

對你來說重要的是什麼，愛情還是金錢？為什麼？

A1: Love is more important to me. Life would be miserable without it. Besides, it's something that you can't buy.

愛情對我來說比較重要。人生如果沒有愛情，會變得很悲慘。此外，愛情是無法用金錢買到的。

A2: I think money is important. I can do lots of wonderful things with it. I can also use it to support the ones I love.

我認為金錢很重要。我可以用它去做很多很棒的事情。我也可以用它去支持我愛的人。

【註】 important〔ɪm'pɔrtn̩t〕adj. 重要的
miserable〔'mɪzərəbl̩〕adj. 悲慘的
besides〔bɪ'saɪdz〕adv. 此外　　*lots of* 很多的
wonderful〔'wʌndəfəl〕adj. 很棒的
support〔sə'port〕v. 支持

4. **Q** : Do you have a hobby?

你有嗜好嗎?

A1: Actually, I have several hobbies. I like to read, watch movies, and play computer games. I also like outdoor activities like basketball and hiking.

事實上,我有好幾個嗜好。我喜歡閱讀、看電影,還有玩電腦遊戲。我也喜歡戶外活動,像是打籃球和健行。

A2: Yes. I play music. I've played the guitar since I was 12 years old. Now I play in a band with some of my friends.

有。我會演奏音樂。我從十二歲起,就開始彈吉他。現在我和一些朋友一起在樂團演奏。

【註】 hobby〔'hɑbɪ〕*n.* 嗜好
actually〔'æktʃuəlɪ〕*adv.* 事實上
several〔'sɛvərəl〕*adj.* 幾個的
outdoor〔'aut،dor〕*adj.* 戶外的
activity〔æk'tɪvətɪ〕*n.* 活動
hiking〔'haɪkɪŋ〕*n.* 健行　　play〔ple〕*v.* 演奏
guitar〔gɪ'tɑr〕*n.* 吉他　　band〔bænd〕*n.* 樂團

5. **Q** : Do you have any secrets?

你有任何祕密嗎?

A1: No, not really. I'm an open book. I tell my friends and family everything.

不,沒有。我是個沒有任何祕密的人。我會告訴我的朋友及家人任何事。

A2: Of course, I do. I think everyone does. It's not a bad thing to have secrets.

我當然有。我覺得每個人都有祕密。有祕密並不是件壞事。

【註】 secret〔'sikrɪt〕*n.* 祕密

not really 事實上不是；沒有

an open book 沒有任何祕密的人   ***of course*** 當然

6. **Q** : Have you ever gotten lost? What did you do? If not, what would you do?

你曾經迷路過嗎？你做了什麼？如果沒有的話，你會怎麼做？

A1: When I was in London, I got separated from my tour group. I had no idea where I was or how to get back to my hotel. I had to ask a police officer for help.

當我在倫敦時，我和我的旅行團走散了。我不知道我在哪裡，或是要如何回到我的飯店。我只好向一名警察求助。

A2: No, I haven't. I have a pretty good sense of direction. So far, I've always been able to find my destination.

不，我不曾迷路過。我的方向感相當好。到目前為止，我總是能找到我的目的地。

【註】 ***get lost*** 迷路   London〔'lʌndən〕*n.* 倫敦

separate〔'sɛpə,ret〕*v.* 使分離

tour group 旅行團   ***have no idea*** 不知道

hotel〔ho'tɛl〕*n.* 飯店

ask sb. for sth. 要求某人某事

police officer 警官；警員

pretty〔'prɪtɪ〕*adv.* 相當   sense〔sɛns〕*n.* 感覺

direction〔 dəˈrɛkʃən 〕n. 方向
sense of direction 方向感　　***so far*** 到目前為止
destination〔ˌdɛstəˈneʃən 〕n. 目的地

7. **Q**：Your friend just lost his dog.　What could you say to him?

你的朋友剛剛弄丟了他的狗。你能對他說什麼？

A1：I'd say, "Don't worry.　He can't have gone far.　I'll help you find him."

我會說：「別擔心。牠不可能走太遠。我會幫你找到牠。」

A2：I'd say, "Let's make a plan.　Let's search block by block.　Do you have a picture of him?"

我會說：「我們來訂個計劃。我們一個街區一個街區地找。你有牠的照片嗎？」

【註】 just〔 dʒʌst 〕*adv.* 剛剛　　lose〔 luz 〕*v.* 遺失
worry〔ˈwɝɪ 〕*v.* 擔心　　plan〔 plæn 〕*n.* 計畫
search〔 sɝtʃ 〕*v.* 尋找；搜尋　　block〔 blɑk 〕*n.* 街區
by〔 baɪ 〕*prep.* （一個）接著（一個）
block by block 一個街區接著一個街區地
picture〔ˈpɪktʃɚ 〕*n.* 照片

＊請將下列自我介紹的句子再唸一遍，請開始。

My seat number is 　(複試座位號碼後 5 碼)　, and my test number is 　(初試准考證號碼後 5 碼)　.

初級英語檢定複試測驗②詳解

寫作能力測驗詳解

第一部份：單句寫作

第1~5題：句子改寫

1. Andrew didn't go to the swimming pool yesterday.

   Andrew never _____.

   　重點結構：never 的用法

   　解　答：<u>Andrew never goes to the swimming pool.</u>

   句型分析：主詞＋never＋動詞＋介系詞＋受詞

   　說　明：由頻率副詞 never（從未）可知，本句為現在式，頻率副詞須置於一般動詞前，又主詞 Andrew 為第三人稱單數，故 go 須改成 goes，並將句尾的 yesterday 去掉。

   * *swimming pool* 游泳池

2. Nathan has lived in Taipei for ten years.

   We _____ in Taipei for ten years.

   　重點結構：單數主詞改為複數主詞

   　解　答：<u>We have lived in Taipei for ten years.</u>

   句型分析：主詞＋have＋過去分詞＋地方副詞＋時間副詞

   　說　明：主詞由第三人稱單數 Nathan 改為複數代名詞 We，所以 has lived 須改為 have lived。

3. Mary is eating lunch now.

Mary will ＿＿＿＿＿＿＿＿＿＿＿＿＿ lunch at one o'clock tomorrow.

　重點結構：現在式改為未來式

　解　答：<u>Mary will eat lunch at one o'clock tomorrow.</u>

　句型分析：主詞＋will＋原形動詞＋時間副詞

　說　明：由提示的 will 和 tomorrow 可知，時態為未來式，故用 will＋原形動詞，所以 eating 須改成 eat。

4. Yes, I can drive a car.

No, I ＿＿＿＿＿＿＿＿＿＿＿＿＿＿＿＿＿＿＿.

　重點結構：肯定回答改為否定回答

　解　答：<u>No, I cannot/can't drive a car.</u>

　句型分析：No＋,＋主詞＋否定助動詞＋原形動詞＋受詞

　說　明：由 No 可知，須接否定句，故 can 改成 cannot 或 can't。

5. Lisa has a sister, doesn't she?

You ＿＿＿＿＿＿＿＿＿＿＿＿＿, ＿＿＿＿＿＿?

　重點結構：第三人稱單數主詞改成 You

　解　答：<u>You have a sister, don't you?</u>

　句型分析：You＋動詞＋受詞＋,＋否定助動詞＋代名詞？

　說　明：主詞由第三人稱單數的 Lisa 改成 You，則附加問句也須由 didn't she? 改成 don't you?。

第 6～10 題：句子合併

6. Rosie doesn't want any coffee.
   Rosie doesn't want any tea.
   Rosie _____ or _____.

　　重點結構：or 的用法

　　　解　答：<u>Rosie doesn't want any coffee or tea.</u>

　　句型分析：主詞＋否定助動詞＋原形動詞＋any＋A＋or＋B

　　　說　明：本句的句意為：「羅西不要任何的咖啡或茶。」
　　　　　　　用 or 連接兩個名詞 coffee 和 tea。

　　* coffee〔ˈkɔfɪ〕*n.* 咖啡

7. The game was cancelled.
   It began to rain.
   _____, so _____.

　　重點結構：so 的用法

　　　解　答：<u>It began to rain, so the game was cancelled.</u>

　　句型分析：主詞＋動詞＋不定詞＋,＋so＋主詞＋be 動詞＋
　　　　　　　過去分詞

　　　說　明：本句的句意為：「開始下起雨，所以比賽被取消
　　　　　　　了。」
　　　　　　　because 和 so 的寫法：
　　　　　　　　　結果＋because＋原因
　　　　　　　　　原因＋so＋結果
　　　　　　　本題為第二種寫法。

　　* game〔gem〕*n.* 比賽　　cancel〔ˈkænsḷ〕*v.* 取消

8. Nicky enjoys playing computer games.
   Nicky enjoys watching movies.
   Nicky _____.

   重點結構：and 的用法
   解　答：Nicky enjoys playing computer games and
   watching movies.
   句型分析：主詞＋enjoys＋動名詞片語 A＋and＋動名詞
   片語 B
   説　明：and 爲對等連接詞，可連接文法地位相同的單字、
   片語或子句，在此連接兩個動名詞片語 playing
   computer games 和 watching movies。

   * enjoy〔ˈɪndʒɔɪ〕v. 喜歡　　*computer game* 電腦遊戲

9. I go to school.
   I eat breakfast.
   _____ before _____.

   重點結構：before 的用法
   解　答：I eat breakfast before I go to school.
   句型分析：主詞＋動詞＋受詞＋before＋主詞＋動詞＋介系詞
   ＋受詞
   説　明：用連接詞 before（在…之前）連接兩句話，表時間
   的先後。本句的句意爲：「我上學之前吃早餐。」

10.　The girl is very happy.

　　The girl won a prize.

　　The girl who _____ happy.

　　　重點結構：who 引導形容詞子句

　　　　解　答：<u>The girl who won a prize is very happy.</u>

　　　句型分析：主詞 + 形容詞子句 + be 動詞 + 副詞 + 形容詞

　　　　説　明：本句的句意爲：「得獎的那個女孩很高興。」

　　　　　　　　who 引導形容詞子句，修飾先行詞 The girl。

　　　* win〔wɪn〕v. 贏得　　　prize〔praɪz〕n. 獎；獎品

第 11～15 題：重組

11.　The _____.

　　on Friday / we / was / movie / saw / great

　　　重點結構：關代當受詞時可省略

　　　　解　答：<u>The movie we saw on Friday was great.</u>

　　　句型分析：主詞 + (關代) + 主詞 + 動詞 + 時間副詞 + be 動詞
　　　　　　　　+ 形容詞

　　　　説　明：本句的句意爲：「我們在星期五看的那部電影很
　　　　　　　　棒。」關代 which 或 that 引導形容詞子句，修飾
　　　　　　　　先行詞 The movie，又關代在子句中當受詞時，
　　　　　　　　可省略。

　　　* great〔gret〕adj. 很棒的

12.　Where _____?

　　your / summer / you / did / vacation / spend

重點結構：問句的基本結構

解　答：<u>Where did you spend your summer vacation?</u>

句型分析：疑問副詞＋助動詞＋主詞＋原形動詞＋受詞？

說　明：本句的句意為：「你在哪裡度過你的暑假？」
疑問副詞 Where（在哪裡）置於句首，助動詞 did
放在主詞 you 前，後接原形動詞 spend，再接受詞
your summer vacation 形成問句。

* spend〔spɛnd〕*v.* 度過　　***summer vacation*** 暑假

13. Nancy ＿＿＿＿＿＿＿＿＿＿＿＿＿＿＿＿＿＿＿＿.
late / never / for / is / work

重點結構：頻率副詞的用法

解　答：<u>Nancy is never late for work.</u>

句型分析：主詞＋be 動詞＋頻率副詞＋形容詞＋介系詞片語

說　明：主詞 Nancy 後須接 be 動詞 is，因為 never（從
不）為頻率副詞，須置於一般動詞前，be 動詞後，
故 is 之後接 never。本句的句意為：「南西上班從
不遲到。」

* late〔let〕*adj.* 遲到的

14. Mark ＿＿＿＿＿＿＿＿＿＿＿＿＿＿＿＿＿＿＿＿.
pencil / buy / to / new / needs / a

重點結構：need 的用法

解　答：<u>Mark needs to buy a new pencil.</u>

句型分析：主詞＋動詞＋不定詞＋受詞

說　明：本句的句意為：「馬克需要買一枝新的鉛筆。」

　　　　need 為一般動詞，其後可接不定詞。

*　need〔nid〕v. 需要

15. I don't like ＿＿＿＿＿＿＿＿＿＿＿＿＿＿＿＿＿＿.

so / hot weather, / I / the summer / don't like

重點結構：so 的用法

解　答：I don't like hot weather, so I don't like the
　　　　summer.

句型分析：主詞＋否定助動詞＋原形動詞＋受詞＋, ＋ so ＋主詞
　　　　　＋否定助動詞＋原形動詞＋受詞

說　明：用連接詞 so 連接兩句話，so（所以）表「結果」。

　　　　本句的句意為：「我不喜歡炎熱的天氣，所以我不
　　　　喜歡夏天。」

*　weather〔'wɛðɚ〕n. 天氣

第二部份：段落寫作

題目： Mr. Wang 嘲笑 Cindy 晴天也帶著傘。請根據以下的圖片寫
　　　　一篇約 50 字的短文。注意：未依提示作答者，將予扣分。

One day, Cindy went for a walk. She carried her umbrella as usual, even though it was a sunny day. Along the way, she met Mr. Wang. He pointed her umbrella and laughed. He thought Cindy was very foolish. *Then suddenly* it began to rain. It rained hard and Mr. Wang was getting wet. Cindy let Mr. Wang share her umbrella, and he decided he would never laugh at others again.

有一天，辛蒂去散步。即使那天的天氣很晴朗，她還是像往常一樣，帶了一把傘。她在路上遇見了王先生。他指著她的傘並且大笑。他認為辛蒂很愚蠢。然後突然間，開始下起雨。雨下得很大，所以王先生就淋濕了。辛蒂讓王先生共用她的傘，而王先生決定了，以後他再也不會嘲笑別人。

one day 有一天   *go for a walk* 去散步
carry〔'kærɪ〕v. 攜帶   umbrella〔ʌm'brɛlə〕n. 雨傘
as usual 像往常一樣   *even though* 即使
sunny〔'sʌnɪ〕adj. 晴朗的   along〔ə'lɔŋ〕prep. 沿著
along the way 在路上   meet〔mit〕v. 遇見
point〔pɔɪnt〕v. 指著   foolish〔'fulɪʃ〕adj. 愚蠢的
suddenly〔'sʌdṇlɪ〕adv. 突然地
hard〔hɑrd〕adv. 猛烈地   *rain hard* 雨下得很大
wet〔wɛt〕adj. 濕的   share〔ʃɛr〕v. 分享；共用
decide〔dɪ'saɪd〕v. 決定   *laugh at* 嘲笑

口説能力測驗詳解

* 請在15秒內完成並唸出下列自我介紹的句子，請開始。

My seat number is （複試座位號碼後5碼），and my test number is （初試准考證號碼後5碼）．

I. 複誦

共五題。題目不印在試卷上，由耳機播出，每題播出兩次，兩次之間大約有一到二秒的間隔。聽完兩次後，請馬上複誦一次。

1. Wait for me here.
   在這裡等我。

2. Is that your car over there?
   在那邊的那一台是你的車嗎？

3. How did you get to the store?
   你如何去那家店？

4. Please close the window. It's too cold.
   請關上窗戶。太冷了。

5. Are the girls sleeping or playing a game?
   那些女孩正在睡覺，還是在玩遊戲？

【註】 *wait for* 等待　　*over there* 在那裡
　　　 get to 到達　　cold〔kold〕*adj.* 寒冷的

II. 朗讀句子與短文

共有五個句子及一篇短文，請先利用一分
鐘的時間閱讀試卷上的句子與短文，然後
在一分鐘內以正常的速度，清楚正確地朗
讀一遍，請開始閱讀。

One　：　The final game, which we won, was the most
　　　　exciting game of the season.
　　　　我們贏了最後那場比賽，那是本季最刺激的比賽。

Two　：　This isn't your new coat, is it?
　　　　這不是你的新外套吧，是嗎？

Three　：　Look at that! Someone is riding a horse on the
　　　　beach.
　　　　看看那個！有人正在海灘上騎馬。

Four　：　What are you going to do tomorrow?
　　　　你明天將會做什麼？

Five　：　Are you happy that your team won the game?
　　　　你們那一隊贏得比賽，你高興嗎？

【註】final〔ˈfaɪnḷ〕adj. 最後的　　game〔gem〕n. 比賽
　　　win〔wɪn〕v. 贏　　exciting〔ɪkˈsaɪtɪŋ〕adj. 刺激的
　　　season〔ˈsizṇ〕n. 季節；時期；（賽）季　　***look at*** 看著
　　　ride〔raɪd〕v. 騎　　horse〔hors〕n. 馬
　　　beach〔bitʃ〕n. 海灘　　team〔tim〕n. 隊

Six   : If you want to avoid painful blisters when you go
        hiking, be sure to break in new shoes first. That
        means you should wear the shoes several times
        before a long hike. This way, the shoes will not be
        too stiff. Also, wear them with the same kind of
        socks that you usually go hiking with.

        當你去健行時，如果想避免疼痛的水泡，你一定要使新
        鞋舒適合腳。意思就是說，在長途健行之前，你應該先
        把新鞋穿過幾次。這樣一來，鞋子就不會太硬。此外，
        穿鞋時要搭配和你平常健行時所穿的同一種襪子。

【註】 avoid〔ə'vɔɪd〕v. 避免
      painful〔'penfəl〕adj. 疼痛的
      blister〔'blɪstə〕n. 水泡
      hike〔haɪk〕v. n. 健行
      be sure to + **V**. 一定要～
      break in 使（鞋或衣服）合用
      mean〔min〕v. 意思是   time〔taɪm〕n. 次
      this way 這樣一來   stiff〔stɪf〕adj. 硬的
      also〔'ɔlso〕adv. 此外   kind〔kaɪnd〕n. 種類
      socks〔saks〕n. pl. 短襪
      usually〔'juʒʊəlɪ〕adv. 通常

Ⅲ. 回答問題

共七題。題目不印在試卷上，由耳機播出，
每題播出兩次，兩次之間大約有一到二秒的
間隔。聽完兩次後，請馬上回答。每題回答
時間為 15 秒，請在作答時間內儘量地表達。

1. **Q**：What did you do before coming to this test today?
   今天來參加測驗之前，你做了什麼？

   A1：This morning I had a big breakfast to give me energy.
   Then I practiced answering English questions with my
   brother. When it was time, I came here.
   今天早上我吃了豐盛的早餐，讓自己有活力。然後我和我
   哥哥練習回答英文問題。當時間一到，我就來這裡了。

   A2：I didn't do anything special. I wanted to relax before
   the test. I slept in and took it easy this morning.
   我沒做什麼特別的事。我想在測驗之前放輕鬆。我今天早
   上起得很晚，並且很放鬆。

   【註】have〔hæv〕v. 吃　　big〔bɪg〕adj. 豐盛的
   energy〔ˈɛnɚdʒɪ〕n. 活力
   practice〔ˈpræktɪs〕v. 練習
   time〔taɪm〕n. 預定的時刻
   special〔ˈspɛʃəl〕adj. 特別的　　relax〔rɪˈlæks〕v. 放鬆
   sleep in 睡到很晚　　**take it easy** 放輕鬆

2. **Q**：Do you have any plans for this weekend?
   你這個週末有任何計劃嗎？

A1: Yes, I do. I'm getting together with some of my friends. We're going to go to a ball game.

是的，我有。我會和一些朋友聚會。我們會去看球賽。

A2: I'm going to spend it with my family. My grandparents are visiting this weekend. We'll have a big dinner together.

我會和家人一起度過。我的祖父母這個週末會來訪。我們會一起吃一頓大餐。

【註】weekend〔'wik‚ɛnd〕*n.* 週末　　***get together*** 聚在一起
ball game 球賽　　spend〔spɛnd〕*v.* 度過
visit〔'vɪzɪt〕*v.* 拜訪

3. **Q** : What's the weather like here in the winter?

這裡的冬天天氣如何？

A1: It's nice and cool. The humidity is lower, too. It's a pleasant time of the year.

天氣很不錯，而且又涼爽。濕度也比較低。那是一年當中最令人愉快的時候。

A2: It's really wet and cold. It rains a lot. I think it's kind of unpleasant.

天氣真的很潮濕又寒冷。常常下雨。我認為天氣有點令人不愉快。

【註】weather〔'wɛðɚ〕*n.* 天氣　　nice〔naɪs〕*adj.* 好的
cool〔kul〕*adj.* 涼爽的
humidity〔hju'mɪdətɪ〕*n.* 濕度
pleasant〔'plɛznt〕*adj.* 令人愉快的
wet〔wɛt〕*adj.* 潮濕的　　***a lot*** 常常

kind of 有點 (= *a little*)
unpleasant〔ʌn'plɛznt〕*adj.* 令人不愉快的

4. **Q** : Who's the tallest person in your family? How tall is he or she?

你們家中最高的人是誰？他或她有多高？

A1: My father is the tallest one. He's 180 centimeters. I wonder if I'll ever be that tall.

我爸爸是最高的。他 180 公分。我想知道自己是否會那麼高。

A2: My older sister is the tallest. She's even a little taller than my father! Surprisingly, she doesn't like to play basketball.

我姐姐是最高的。她甚至比我爸爸還要高一點！令人驚訝的是，她不喜歡打籃球。

【註】centimeter〔'sɛntə,mitɚ〕*n.* 公分
wonder〔'wʌndɚ〕*v.* 想知道
ever〔'ɛvɚ〕*adv.* 究竟；到底
surprisingly〔sə'praɪzɪŋlɪ〕*adv.* 令人驚訝的是

5. **Q** : Which do you like better, traveling alone or traveling with other people?

你比較喜歡哪一個，獨自旅行或和其他人一起旅行？

A1: I prefer to travel with other people. I think it's more fun to share the experience with someone. Besides that, it's a lot safer.

　　我比較喜歡和其他人一起旅行。我認為和人分享經驗比較
有趣。此外，這樣也安全多了。

A2: I like to travel by myself. I want to be free to do the
things I like. I think it's also a challenge and good
training for me.

　　我喜歡獨自旅行。我想要自由地做我喜歡的事。我認為這
對我而言也是一種挑戰，而且是很好的訓練。

【註】 *like better* 比較喜歡　　alone〔ə'lon〕*adv.* 獨自
prefer〔prɪ'fɝ〕*v.* 比較喜歡　　fun〔fʌn〕*adj.* 有趣的
share〔ʃɛr〕*v.* 分享　　experience〔ɪk'spɪrɪəns〕*n.* 經驗
besides〔bɪ'saɪdz〕*prep.* 除了…之外 (還有)
safe〔sef〕*adj.* 安全的　　*by oneself* 獨自
free〔fri〕*adj.* 自由的　　challenge〔'tʃælɪndʒ〕*n.* 挑戰
training〔'trenɪŋ〕*n.* 訓練

6. **Q** : Have you ever lost something important to you?
　　你曾經遺失對你而言很重要的東西嗎？

A1: Sure. I lost my wallet once. That caused me a lot of
trouble. All of my ID and credit cards were in it.

　　當然。我曾經遺失我的皮夾。那造成我很多的麻煩。我所
有的證件和信用卡都在裡面。

A2: Yes. Once I lost a ring. It was a gift from my first
girlfriend. It had a lot of sentimental value, and I felt
terrible about it.

　　有。有一次我遺失了一個戒指。那是我初戀女友送我的禮
物。它很有紀念價值，所以我覺得很難過。

【註】 ever〔'ɛvɚ〕*adv.* 曾經　　lose〔luz〕*v.* 遺失

important〔ɪmˈpɔrtn̩t〕adj. 重要的

sure〔ʃur〕adv. 當然　　wallet〔ˈwɑlɪt〕n. 皮夾

once〔wʌns〕adv. 曾經　　cause〔kɔz〕v. 造成

ID 身份證（= ID card）　　***credit card*** 信用卡

ring〔rɪŋ〕n. 戒指　　girlfriend〔ˈgɝl,frɛnd〕n. 女朋友

sentimental〔ˌsɛntəˈmɛntl̩〕adj. 情感的

value〔ˈvælju〕n. 價值

terrible〔ˈtɛrəbl̩〕adj. 糟糕的；難受的

7. **Q**：Your sister asks you to do her a favor, but you don't want to do it. What can you say to her?

你姐姐請你幫她一個忙，但你不想幫。你能對她說什麼？

A1：I'd say, "I'd like to help you out, Sis. But I just can't do it. Why don't you ask Mom or Dad for help?"

我會說：「我想要幫助妳，姐姐。但我就是沒辦法。妳何不請爸爸或媽媽幫忙？」

A2：I think I'd say, "I'm sorry, but I can't do it. I'm really busy right now. If I can help you later, let me know."

我想我會說：「很抱歉，我做不到。我現在真的很忙。如果我可以待會再幫妳，要讓我知道。」

【註】***do*** *sb.* ***a favor*** 幫某人一個忙　　***help*** *sb.* ***out*** 幫忙某人 sis〔sɪs〕n. 姐姐；妹妹　　***ask*** *sb.* ***for help*** 向某人求助 ***right now*** 現在　　later〔ˈletɚ〕adv. 待會

* 請將下列自我介紹的句子再唸一遍，請開始。

My seat number is （複試座位號碼後 5 碼）, and my test

number is （初試准考證號碼後 5 碼）.

初級英語檢定複試測驗③詳解

寫作能力測驗詳解

第一部份：單句寫作

第1～5題：句子改寫

1. There is an egg in the refrigerator.

    There aren't ＿＿＿＿＿＿＿＿＿＿＿ in the refrigerator.

    重點結構：there is/are 的用法

    解　答：<u>There aren't any eggs in the refrigerator.</u>

    句型分析：There ＋ aren't ＋ any ＋ 複數名詞 ＋ 地方副詞

    説　明：there is/are 表「有」，依提示，是將肯定改爲否定，且單數的 is 改成複數的 are，故須用複數名詞，將 an egg 改成 any eggs。not any（沒有任何的）等於 no。本句的句意爲：「冰箱裡沒有任何的蛋。」

    * refrigerator〔rɪˈfrɪdʒəˌretə〕*n.* 冰箱

2. Yes, I brought my notebook to school.

    No, I ＿＿＿＿＿＿＿＿＿＿＿ my notebook to school.

    重點結構：肯定回答改成否定回答

    解　答：<u>No, I didn't bring my notebook to school.</u>

    句型分析：No ＋ , ＋ 主詞 ＋ 否定助動詞 ＋ 原形動詞 ＋ 受詞 ＋ 副詞片語

說　明：肯定改成否定，又依句意為過去式，故用 didn't，
再接原形動詞，故 brought 須改成 bring。本句的
句意為：「不，我沒有帶我的筆記本去學校。」

* notebook〔'not,buk〕*n.* 筆記本

3. John is running in the park now.
   The students ＿＿＿＿＿＿＿＿＿＿＿＿＿＿＿＿＿＿ now.

　重點結構：單數主詞改為複數主詞
　　解　答：The students are running in the park now.
　句型分析：主詞＋be 動詞＋現在分詞＋地方副詞＋時間副詞
　　說　明：主詞由單數 John 改為複數 The students，故 be 動
　　　　　　詞也須由 is 改成 are。本句的句意為：「那些學生
　　　　　　現在正在公園裡跑步。」

4. Yes, you must come to school on Friday.
   No, you don't ＿＿＿＿＿＿＿＿＿＿＿＿＿＿＿ on Friday.

　重點結構：must 的用法
　　解　答：No, you don't have to come to school on Friday.
　句型分析：No＋,＋主詞＋否定助動詞＋原形動詞＋介系詞＋
　　　　　　受詞＋時間副詞
　　說　明：助動詞 must 的否定，有兩種寫法：
　　　　　　① mustn't「絕對禁止」。
　　　　　　② don't have to「不必」。
　　　　　　依句意為第二種用法。
　　　　　　本句的句意為：「不，你星期五不必來學校。」

5. I will visit my grandmother today.

I _____ yesterday.

　重點結構：未來式改成過去式

　解　答：<u>I visited my grandmother yesterday.</u>

　句型分析：主詞＋動詞＋受詞＋時間副詞

　說　明：由 yesterday 可知，本句為過去式，故 will visit
　　　　　須改為 visited。本句的句意為：「我昨天去探望
　　　　　我的祖母。」

　＊ visit〔ˋvɪzɪt〕v. 拜訪；探望
　　 grandmother〔ˋgrænd͵mʌðɚ〕n. 祖母

第 6～10 題：句子合併

6. George walked slowly.

He was late for school.

George _____ so _____ that _____.

　重點結構：so…that 的用法

　解　答：<u>George walked so slowly that he was late for
　　　　　school.</u>

　句型分析：主詞＋動詞＋so＋副詞＋that＋主詞＋be 動詞＋
　　　　　形容詞＋介系詞片語

　說　明：so…that 表「如此…以致於」。本句的句意為：
　　　　　「喬治走得如此地慢，以致於他上學遲到了。」
　　　　　副詞 so 修飾副詞 slowly，that 引導表結果的副
　　　　　詞子句，修飾前面的相關副詞 so。

　＊ slowly〔ˋslolɪ〕adv. 慢地　　late〔let〕adj. 遲到的

7. My dog is cute.

My dog is very naughty.

My dog ＿＿＿＿＿＿＿＿＿＿＿ but ＿＿＿＿＿＿＿＿＿＿＿.

> 重點結構：but 的用法
>
> 解　答：<u>My dog is cute but (it is) very naughty.</u>
>
> 句型分析：主詞＋be 動詞＋形容詞＋but＋副詞＋形容詞
>
> 説　明：but 爲表反義的對等連接詞，連接文法地位相同的
> 單字、片語或子句，在此連接兩個形容詞 cute 和
> very naughty。本句的句意爲：「我的狗很可愛，
> 但非常頑皮。」
>
> * cute〔kut〕*adj.* 可愛的
> naughty〔'nɔtɪ〕*adj.* 頑皮的

8. Peter likes pizza.

Peter likes noodles the best.

Peter likes ＿＿＿＿＿＿＿＿＿＿＿ better ＿＿＿＿＿＿＿＿＿＿.

> 重點結構：like…better than 的用法
>
> 解　答：<u>Peter likes noodles better than pizza.</u>
>
> 句型分析：主詞＋動詞＋受詞 A＋better than＋受詞 B
>
> 説　明：like…better 作「比較喜歡…」解，又 better 爲比
> 較級，連接詞須用 than。本句的句意爲：「彼得喜
> 歡披薩。」「彼得最喜歡麵。」也就是「彼得喜歡
> 麵甚於披薩。」
>
> * pizza〔'pitsə〕*n.* 披薩　　noodles〔'nudḷz〕*n. pl.* 麵

9. Mr. Brown has a car.

The car's roof is yellow.

Mr. Brown ＿＿＿＿＿＿＿＿＿＿＿ whose ＿＿＿＿＿＿＿＿＿＿.

　　重點結構：whose 的用法

　　　解　答：Mr. Brown has a car whose roof is yellow.

　　句型分析：主詞＋動詞＋受詞＋whose＋名詞＋be 動詞＋
　　　　　　　形容詞

　　　說　明：本句的句意為：「布朗先生有一輛車頂是黃色的汽
　　　　　　　車。」用關代所有格 whose 引導形容詞子句，修飾
　　　　　　　先行詞 car。

　　＊ roof〔ruf〕n. 屋頂；（汽車的）車頂

10. My bag is not here.

My bag is blue.

My ＿＿＿＿＿＿＿＿＿＿＿＿＿＿＿＿＿＿＿＿＿＿＿＿.

　　重點結構：句子的基本結構

　　　解　答：My blue bag is not here.

　　句型分析：主詞＋be 動詞＋not＋副詞

　　　說　明：本句的句意為：「我的藍色袋子不在這裡。」形容
　　　　　　　詞 blue 修飾名詞 bag。

第 11～15 題：重組

11. Have ＿＿＿＿＿＿＿＿＿＿＿＿＿＿＿＿＿＿＿＿＿＿＿？

Germany / you / been / to / ever

重點結構：have ever been to 的用法

解　答：<u>Have you ever been to Germany?</u>

句型分析：Have ＋ 主詞 ＋ ever ＋ been ＋ to ＋ 地名？

說　明：have ever been to 表「曾經去過」，因為是疑問
句，所以 Have 置於句首，再寫主詞 you，再加
ever been to，最後再接地點 Germany（德國）。
本句的句意為：「你曾經去過德國嗎？」

* ever〔ˈɛvɚ〕adv. 曾經　　Germany〔ˈdʒɝmənɪ〕n. 德國

12. Don't ————————————————————.
to / the trash / take out / forget

重點結構：forget 的用法

解　答：<u>Don't forget to take out the trash.</u>

句型分析：Don't ＋ forget ＋ to V. ＋ 受詞

說　明：本句的句意為：「不要忘記把垃圾拿出去。」
forget 的寫法有兩種：

> forget to V. 忘記去做～【動作未完成】
> forget V-ing 忘記做過～【動作已完成】

本句為第一種寫法。

* trash〔træʃ〕n. 垃圾
take out the trash 把垃圾拿出去；倒垃圾

13. Steve ————————————————————.
ever / watches / in the evening / hardly / TV

重點結構：hardly ever 的用法

解　答：<u>Steve hardly ever watches TV in the evening.</u>

句型分析：主詞＋hardly ever＋動詞＋受詞＋時間副詞

說　明：副詞片語 hardly ever（很少）修飾動詞 watches。

本句的句意為：「史蒂夫很少在晚上看電視。」

14. It might ＿＿＿＿＿＿＿＿＿＿＿＿＿＿＿＿＿＿＿.

take / , so / I / rain / will / my / umbrella

重點結構：so 的用法

解　答：<u>It might rain, so I will take my umbrella.</u>

句型分析：主詞＋might＋原形動詞＋,＋so＋主詞＋will＋
原形動詞＋受詞

說　明：so（所以）為表「結果」的對等連接詞，連接兩句
話。本句的句意為：「可能會下雨，所以我會帶我
的雨傘。」

15. The ＿＿＿＿＿＿＿＿＿＿＿＿＿＿＿＿＿＿＿＿.

Margaret / was / cake / delicious / that / made

重點結構：關係代名詞 that 的用法

解　答：<u>The cake that Margaret made was delicious.</u>

句型分析：主詞＋形容詞子句＋be 動詞＋形容詞

說　明：關代 that 引導形容詞子句，修飾先行詞 The cake。
本句的句意為：「瑪格麗特做的蛋糕很好吃。」

* delicious〔dɪˈlɪʃəs〕adj. 好吃的

第二部份：段落寫作

題目：Dan 因為做了一個很醜的花瓶而受挫。請根據以下的圖片寫
一篇約 50 字的短文。注意：未依提示作答者，將予扣分。

One day in art class, Dan and his friends were making
vases. Everyone was able to make a simple vase except
Dan. ***No matter*** how hard he tried, it was ugly. He looked
at his friends' vases and tried again. He did not give up. To
everyone's surprise, Dan was able to make the most beautiful
vase of all! Everyone in class clapped for him loudly.

　有一天在上美術課時，丹和他的朋友正在做花瓶。每個人都能
夠做出一個簡單的花瓶，除了丹以外。無論他多努力嘗試，就是很
醜。他看著朋友的花瓶，又試了一次。他並沒有放棄。令大家驚訝
的是，丹能夠做出所有的花瓶中，最漂亮的一個！班上的每個人都
為他大聲地鼓掌。

art〔ɑrt〕*n.* 藝術　　　vase〔ves〕*n.* 花瓶
be able to V. 能夠…　　simple〔'sɪmpl̩〕*adj.* 簡單的
except〔ɪk'sɛpt〕*prep.* 除了…之外
no matter how hard 無論多麼地努力　　try〔traɪ〕*v.* 嘗試
ugly〔'ʌglɪ〕*adj.* 醜的　　***look at*** 看著　　***give up*** 放棄
to one's surprise 令某人驚訝的是　　***in class*** 在班上
clap〔klæp〕*v.* 鼓掌　　loudly〔'laʊdlɪ〕*adv.* 大聲地

口說能力測驗詳解

＊請在 15 秒內完成並唸出下列自我介紹的句子，請開始。

My seat number is (複試座位號碼後 5 碼) , and my test number is (初試准考證號碼後 5 碼) .

I. 複誦

共五題。題目不印在試卷上，由耳機播出，
每題播出兩次，兩次之間大約有一到二秒的
間隔。聽完兩次後，請馬上複誦一次。

1. Is Amanda's hair long or short?
   阿曼達的頭髮是長的還是短的？

2. Relax.　We have plenty of time.
   放輕鬆。我們有很多時間。

3. Who is standing next to Bill?
   誰正站在比爾的旁邊？

4. Are these your suitcases?　這些是你的手提箱嗎？

5. Please open the window.　請打開窗戶。

【註】 hair〔hɛr〕n. 頭髮　　relax〔rɪˋlæks〕v. 放鬆
　　　plenty of 很多的　　**next to** 在⋯隔壁；在⋯旁邊
　　　suitcase〔ˋsut͵kes〕n. 手提箱

II. 朗讀句子與短文

共有五個句子及一篇短文，請先利用一分
鐘的時間閱讀試卷上的句子與短文，然後
在一分鐘內以正常的速度，清楚正確地朗
讀一遍，請開始閱讀。

One　　：　Have you been to this café before?

你以前去過這家咖啡廳嗎？

Two　　：　The boy who left the box didn't say who it was
　　　　　from.

留下這個箱子的男孩並沒說這是誰送的。

Three　：　How long have you been working on this project?

你做這個計劃多久了？

Four　　：　Please open the door for me.

請替我把門打開。

Five　　：　You didn't talk to Nancy, did you?

你沒跟南西說話，是嗎？

【註】　*have been to* 去過　　café〔kə`fe〕*n.* 咖啡廳
leave〔liv〕*v.* 留下　　*work on* 致力於
project〔`pradʒɛkt〕*n.* 計劃

Six : Many people have had their bikes stolen, but there are some ways you can prevent it. First, try to lock your bike to something inside. If you have to leave it outside, make sure that the area is open and well-lit. It's also a good idea to park it near bikes that look more expensive than yours!

許多人都曾經被偷過腳踏車，但有一些方法可以預防。首先，試著把你的腳踏車鎖在室內的某樣東西上。如果你必須把它留在外面，那就要確定那個地區是空曠而且光線充足。把它停在看起來比你的貴很多的腳踏車附近，也是個好主意！

【註】 bike〔baɪk〕n. 腳踏車（= bicycle）
steal〔stil〕v. 偷【三態變化：steal-stole-stolen】
way〔we〕n. 方法　　prevent〔prɪˋvɛnt〕v. 預防
lock〔lɑk〕v. 鎖　　inside〔ˋɪnˋsaɪd〕adv. 在室內
outside〔ˋautˋsaɪd〕adv. 在外面
make sure 確定　　area〔ˋɛrɪə〕n. 地區
open〔ˋopən〕adj. 開闊的；空曠的
light〔laɪt〕v. 給…點燈；使…明亮【三態變化：light-lit-lit】
well-lit〔ˋwɛlˏlɪt〕adj. 明亮的；光線充足的
park〔pɑrk〕v. 停（車）
expensive〔ɪkˋspɛnsɪv〕adj. 昂貴的

III. 回答問題

共七題。題目不印在試卷上，由耳機播出，
每題播出兩次，兩次之間大約有一到二秒的
間隔。聽完兩次後，請馬上回答。每題回答
時間爲 15 秒，請在作答時間內儘量地表達。

1. **Q** : How was your trip to the test center today?
　　　今天你來測驗中心的路程如何？

　　A1: It was fine.　I found out where it was in advance.　I
　　　didn't have any problems on the way.
　　　很好。我事先就查明它的位置。一路上沒有任何問題。

　　A2: It didn't take as long as I thought.　I got here nearly an
　　　hour early.　Better safe than sorry, though.
　　　花費的時間並沒有我想的那麼久。我幾乎一個小時前就到
　　　這裡。不過，安全總比後悔好。

　　【註】 trip〔trɪp〕n. 行程　　center〔'sɛntɚ〕n. 中心
　　　　　find out 查明　　*in advance* 事先
　　　　　on the way 一路上　　take〔tek〕v. 花費
　　　　　nearly〔'nɪrlɪ〕adv. 幾乎
　　　　　Better safe than sorry.【諺】安全總比後悔好。
　　　　　though〔ðo〕adv.【置於句尾】不過

2. **Q** : Have you ever told someone you were sorry?
　　　What was the reason?
　　　你曾經跟人說過你很抱歉嗎？原因是什麼？

　　A1: Yes, I have.　I said that to my mother.　I had broken
　　　something of hers.
　　　是的，我有。我對我媽媽說過。我打破了她的某樣東西。

A2: Not that I can remember. Of course, I do wrong
things. But my family and friends always forgive me
right away.

我不記得有。當然，我會做錯事。但我的家人和朋友總是
立刻就原諒我。

【註】 reason〔'rizn̩〕*n.* 原因　　break〔brek〕*v.* 打破
Not that I can remember. 我不記得有。(= *No, I don't
remember anything like that happening.*)
of course 當然　　wrong〔rɔŋ〕*adj.* 錯誤的
forgive〔fə'gɪv〕*v.* 原諒　　***right away*** 立刻

3. **Q** ： What is the weather like here in the summer?
這裡的夏天天氣如何？

A1: It's very hot and humid. Some people find it pretty
uncomfortable. It's best to stay in some place that's
air-conditioned.

非常炎熱而且潮濕。有些人覺得相當不舒服。最好是待在
某個有空調的地方。

A2: It's usually hot and sunny. But sometimes we get
typhoons. On those days we have a lot of rain and
very strong winds.

通常炎熱又晴朗。但有時我們會有颱風。在那樣的日子，
會下很多雨，而且有很強的風。

【註】 weather〔'wɛðə〕*n.* 天氣
humid〔'hjumɪd〕*adj.* 潮濕的　　find〔faɪnd〕*v.* 覺得
pretty〔'prɪtɪ〕*adv.* 相當
uncomfortable〔ʌn'kʌmfətəbl̩〕*adj.* 不舒服的
stay〔ste〕*v.* 停留；待在　　some〔sʌm〕*adj.* 某個
air-conditioned〔'ɛrkən,dɪʃənd〕*adj.* 有空調的

usually〔ˈjuʒʊəlɪ〕 *adv.* 通常　　sunny〔ˈsʌnɪ〕 *adj.* 晴朗的
typhoon〔taɪˈfun〕 *n.* 颱風　　wind〔wɪnd〕 *n.* 風

4. **Q**： What are you interested in outside of school or work?
　　不上學或不上班時，你對什麼有興趣？

A1： I really like sports. I watch basketball and baseball on TV. I also play basketball on weekends.
我很喜歡運動。我會看電視上的籃球和棒球。我週末時也會打籃球。

A2： I'm into music. I sometimes go to concerts or clubs to hear it. I also have a pretty big music collection at home.
我很喜歡音樂。我有時會去音樂會或俱樂部聽音樂。我在家也有相當大批的音樂收藏品。

【註】 interested〔ˈɪntrɪstɪd〕 *adj.* 有興趣的 < *in* >
outside of school or work 不上學或不上班時（= *when you're not in school or at work*）
sport〔sport〕 *n.* 運動　　***on weekends*** 在週末
be into 對⋯很感興趣；很喜歡
concert〔ˈkɑnsɝt〕 *n.* 音樂會；演唱會
club〔klʌb〕 *n.* 俱樂部
collection〔kəˈlɛkʃən〕 *n.* （一批）收藏品

5. **Q**： Which do you like better, traveling by bus or traveling by train?
　　你比較喜歡哪一個，搭巴士旅行還是搭火車旅行？

A1： I like traveling by bus better. In most cases, they run more frequently and go to more places. I also get to see the beautiful mountain scenery instead of a bunch of tunnels.

我比較喜歡搭巴士旅行。在大部份的情況中，它們的班次
較頻繁，而且去的地方比較多。我也能看到漂亮的山景，
而不是一堆隧道。

A2: Oh, I much prefer going by train.　There's more room
to spread out, so it's more comfortable.　I also think
it's safer than being on the highway.

喔，我眞的比較喜歡搭火車去旅行。有更多的空間可以伸
展，所以比較舒適。我也認爲這比在公路上安全。

【註】case〔kes〕*n.* 情況　　run〔rʌn〕*v.* 行駛
frequently〔'frikwəntlɪ〕*adv.* 經常；頻繁地
get to V. 得以…　　scenery〔'sinərɪ〕*n.* 風景
instead of 而不是　　bunch〔bʌntʃ〕*n.* 束；串；一大堆
tunnel〔'tʌnl̩〕*n.* 隧道　　prefer〔prɪ'fɝ〕*v.* 比較喜歡
room〔rum〕*n.* 空間　　spread〔sprɛd〕*v.* 伸展（四肢）
highway〔'haɪ,we〕*n.* 公路

6. **Q**：Have you ever met a famous person?
你曾經遇過名人嗎？

A1: I met a famous basketball player once.　He came to
our school to give a talk.　Afterwards, he signed my
basketball and shook my hand.

我曾經見過一位著名的籃球選手。他來我們學校演講。之
後，他在我的籃球上簽名，並和我握手。

A2: No, I've never met anyone famous.　But I'm not very
interested in talking to celebrities anyway.　I think
they're just people like you and me.

沒有，我從未遇過任何有名的人。但反正我對和名人說話
並不是很有興趣。我認爲他們只是像你我一樣的人。

【註】meet〔mit〕*v.* 遇見；和…會面

famous (ˈfeməs) *adj.* 有名的
player (ˈpleɚ) *n.* 球員；選手　　***give a talk*** 發表演說
afterwards (ˈæftɚwɚdz) *adv.* 之後
sign (saɪn) *v.* 在…簽名
shake *one's* ***hand*** 握某人的手
celebrity (səˈlɛbrətɪ) *n.* 名人
anyway (ˈɛnɪ,we) *adv.* 反正　　like (laɪk) *prep.* 像

7. **Q** : A stranger asks you for directions, but you don't know the answer.　What can you say to him?
   有個陌生人向你問路，但你不知道答案。你能對他說什麼？

A1: I'd tell him the truth.　I'd say, "I'm sorry, but I don't know.　I think you should ask somebody else."
   我會告訴他實話。我會說：「很抱歉，我不知道。我認為你應該問別人。」

A2: I'd say, "I'm sorry, but I can't help you.　I've never heard of that place.　Why don't we ask this shopkeeper?"
   我會說：「很抱歉，我無法幫你。我從未聽過那個地方。我們何不問這一位老闆？」

【註】 stranger (ˈstrendʒɚ) *n.* 陌生人
　　　directions (dəˈrɛkʃənz) *n. pl.* (行路的) 指引
　　　truth (truθ) *n.* 實話　　else (ɛls) *adj.* 其他的
　　　hear of 聽說　　shopkeeper (ˈʃɑp,kipɚ) *n.* 店主；老闆

* 請將下列自我介紹的句子再唸一遍，請開始。

My seat number is (複試座位號碼後 5 碼) , and my test number is (初試准考證號碼後 5 碼) .

初級英語檢定複試測驗④詳解

寫作能力測驗詳解

第一部份：單句寫作

第1~5題：句子改寫

1. I play basketball every Saturday.

   David _____.

   > 重點結構：主詞由第一人稱改爲第三人稱單數
   >
   > 解　　答：David plays basketball every Saturday.
   >
   > 句型分析：主詞＋動詞＋受詞＋時間副詞
   >
   > 説　　明：主詞由 I 改爲第三人稱單數的 David，動詞須由 play 改爲 plays。本句的句意爲：「大衛每個星期六都會打籃球。」
   >
   > * basketball〔'bæskɪtˌbɔl〕n. 籃球

2. Yes, Nancy went to the library yesterday.

   No, Nancy _____ to the library yesterday.

   > 重點結構：肯定回答改爲否定回答
   >
   > 解　　答：No, Nancy didn't go to the library yesterday.
   >
   > 句型分析：No＋,＋主詞＋否定助動詞＋動詞片語＋時間副詞
   >
   > 説　　明：肯定回答改爲否定，故將 Yes 改成 No，又過去式動詞 went to 須改成 didn't go to。本句的句意爲：「不，南西昨天沒有去圖書館。」
   >
   > * library〔'laɪˌbrɛrɪ〕n. 圖書館

3. When does the store open?

Tell me _____.

重點結構：間接問句的用法

解　答：<u>Tell me when the store opens.</u>

句型分析：Tell＋受詞＋疑問副詞＋主詞＋動詞

説　明：tell *sb. sth.*「告訴某人某事」，tell 接間接受詞
（人）之後，須接直接受詞（事），故須將疑問句
改成名詞子句，即「疑問副詞＋主詞＋動詞」的形
式。本句的句意為：「告訴我那間商店何時開。」

4. My friend Susan is in the guitar club.

I _____.

重點結構：主詞由第三人稱單數改為第一人稱

解　答：<u>I am in the guitar club.</u>

句型分析：主詞＋be 動詞＋地方副詞

説　明：本句的句意為：「我是吉他社的。」將 My friend
Susan 改為 I，故 be 動詞須由 is 改成 am。

* guitar〔gɪˈtɑr〕*n.* 吉他　　club〔klʌb〕*n.* 俱樂部；社團

5. Peter rode his bike to school yesterday.

Peter _____ now.

重點結構：過去式改為現在進行式

解　答：<u>Peter is riding his bike to school now.</u>

句型分析：主詞＋be 動詞＋V-ing＋受詞＋介系詞片語＋時間
副詞

說　明：本句的句意為：「彼得現在正騎著他的腳踏車去上學。」過去式改為現在進行式，過去式動詞 rode 須改為 is riding。

第 6～10 題：句子合併

6. Would you like to drink coffee?

Would you like to drink tea?

Would ＿＿＿＿＿＿＿＿＿＿＿＿＿＿＿＿＿＿＿ tea?

重點結構：or 的用法

解　答：<u>Would you like to drink coffee or tea?</u>

句型分析：Would you like to + 原形動詞 + 受詞 A + or + 受詞 B？

說　明：本句的句意為：「你想要喝咖啡或是茶？」用表「選擇」的對等連接詞 or，連接兩個名詞 coffee 和 tea。

* *would like to V.* 想要…　　coffee〔ˈkɔfɪ〕*n.* 咖啡

7. This is my book.

I like this book the best.

＿＿＿＿＿＿＿＿＿＿＿＿＿ favorite ＿＿＿＿＿＿＿＿＿＿＿．

重點結構：favorite 的用法

解　答：<u>This is my favorite book.</u>

句型分析：This + be 動詞 + 所有格形容詞 + 形容詞 + 名詞

說　明：like better 是「比較喜歡」，like…the best 是「最喜歡…」，寫成形容詞則是 favorite「最喜

愛的」，用來修飾名詞 book。本句的句意爲：
「這是我最喜愛的書。」

8. This is my brother.

My brother goes to National Taiwan University.

This _____ who _____.

重點結構：關係代名詞 who 的用法

解　答：<u>This is my brother who goes to National Taiwan University.</u>

句型分析：指示代名詞＋be 動詞＋名詞（先行詞）＋形容詞子句

説　明：本句的句意爲：「這位是我就讀國立台灣大學的哥哥。」用表「人」的關代 who 引導形容詞子句，修飾先行詞 my brother。

* **go to** 就讀　　national〔'næʃənḷ〕adj. 國立的
university〔ˌjunə'vɝsətɪ〕n. 大學

9. Take out the garbage at 9:00.

Don't forget it.

Don't _____.

重點結構：forget 的用法

解　答：<u>Don't forget to take out the garbage at 9:00.</u>

句型分析：Don't＋forget＋不定詞＋受詞＋時間副詞

説　明：本句的句意爲：「不要忘記九點要倒垃圾。」

forget（忘記）的寫法有兩種：

⎧ forget V-ing 忘記做過…【動作已完成】
⎩ forget to V. 忘記去做…【動作未完成】

本題為第二種寫法。

* forget〔fɚˋgɛt〕v. 忘記　　garbage〔ˋgɑrbɪdʒ〕n. 垃圾
take out the garbage 把垃圾拿出去；倒垃圾

10. John has a dog and a cat.
The dog is brown.
John _____ cat.

重點結構：形容詞修飾名詞
解　答：<u>John has a brown dog and a cat.</u>
句型分析：主詞＋動詞＋受詞 A＋and＋受詞 B
說　明：本句的句意為：「約翰有一隻棕色的狗和一隻貓。」
brown（棕色的）是形容詞，放在所修飾的名詞
dog 前。

第 11～15 題：重組

11. What _____?
you / on the weekend / do / usually / do

重點結構：疑問句的結構
解　答：<u>What do you usually do on the weekend?</u>
句型分析：What＋do＋you＋頻率副詞＋原形動詞＋時間
副詞？

説　明：本句的句意為：「你在週末通常會做什麼？」疑問
代名詞 What 置於句首，後接助動詞 do，再接主詞
you，形成倒裝，再加頻率副詞 usually（通常）之
後，再接原形動詞 do（做），時間副詞 on the
weekend（在週末）則置於句尾。

* usually〔ˈjuʒʊəlɪ〕adv. 通常　　weekend〔ˈwikˌɛnd〕n. 週末

12. The _____.
annoying / dog / all night / barks / is / that

重點結構：關代 that 的用法
解　答：The dog that barks all night is annoying.
句型分析：主詞＋形容詞子句＋be 動詞＋形容詞
説　明：本句的句意為：「那隻整晚都在吠叫的狗很令人心
煩。」關代 that 引導形容詞子句，修飾先行詞 The
dog。

* bark〔bɑrk〕v. 吠叫
annoying〔əˈnɔɪɪŋ〕adj. 令人心煩的

13. Today _____.
don't have to / we / Sunday, / go / so / to school / is

重點結構：so 的用法
解　答：Today is Sunday, so we don't have to go to
school.
句型分析：主詞＋be 動詞＋補語＋，＋so＋主詞＋否定助動詞
＋have to＋原形動詞

　説　　明：本句的句意為：「今天是星期天，所以我們不必去
　　　　　　　上學。」so（所以）的用法為：原因，so＋結果。
　　　　　　　Today is Sunday 是原因，we don't have to go
　　　　　　　to school 是結果。

14. I _____ in the park.
often / play / don't / basketball

　重點結構：頻率副詞 often 的用法

　解　　答：I don't often play basketball in the park.

　句型分析：主詞＋否定助動詞＋頻率副詞＋原形動詞＋受詞＋
　　　　　　　地方副詞

　説　　明：本句的句意為：「我們不常在公園裡打籃球。」
　　　　　　　頻率副詞 often 須放在 be 動詞後，一般動詞前。

15. The _____.
books / forgot / boys / their / to bring

　重點結構：句子的基本結構

　解　　答：The boys forgot to bring their books.

　句型分析：主詞＋動詞＋不定詞＋受詞

　説　　明：本句的句意為：「那些男孩忘了帶他們的書。」
　　　　　　　定冠詞 The 須接名詞，依句意，應是「男孩」忘了
　　　　　　　帶「書」，所以主詞是 The boys，依句意為過去
　　　　　　　式，故「忘了帶」用 forgot to bring，再接 their
　　　　　　　books。

第二部份：段落寫作

題目： Mr. Lee 因工作疲累，而接受同事建議。請根據以下的圖片
寫一篇約 50 字的短文。**注意**：未依提示作答者，將予扣分。

Mr. Lee was working late at his office. He still had a lot of reports to finish and it was already 3:00 a.m. He was very tired. Mr. Lee's colleague offered to bring him a cup of coffee. This made Mr. Lee very happy. ***But then*** the colleague spilled the coffee all over Mr. Lee's desk! ***Then*** poor Mr. Lee had even more work to do.

　　李先生在他的辦公室工作到很晚。他還有很多報告要完成，而時間已經是凌晨三點。他非常疲倦。李先生的同事提議要拿一杯咖啡給他。這使得李先生非常高興。不過後來那位同事把咖啡全灑在李先生的辦公桌上！然後可憐的李先生，就有更多的工作要做。

late〔 let 〕*adv.* 到很晚；到深夜　　　report〔 rɪˈport 〕*n.* 報告
finish〔ˈfɪnɪʃ〕*v.* 完成　　　tired〔 taɪrd 〕*adj.* 疲倦的
colleague〔ˈkɑlig〕*n.* 同事　　　offer〔ˈɔfɚ〕*v.* 提議
spill〔 spɪl 〕*v.* 灑出　　　***all over*** 遍及；在…到處
desk〔 dɛsk 〕*n.* 辦公桌　　　poor〔 pur 〕*adj.* 可憐的
even〔ˈivən〕*adv.* 更加

口説能力測驗詳解

*請在15秒內完成並唸出下列自我介紹的句子，請開始。

My seat number is <u>（複試座位號碼後 5 碼）</u>, and my test number is <u>（初試准考證號碼後 5 碼）</u>.

I. 複誦

共五題。題目不印在試卷上，由耳機播出，
每題播出兩次，兩次之間大約有一到二秒的
間隔。聽完兩次後，請馬上複誦一次。

1. Are you going swimming tomorrow?
   你明天會去游泳嗎？

2. You can put your coat over there.
   你可以把你的外套放在那裡。

3. Where did you go on your last vacation?
   你上次休假是去哪裡？

4. Be careful. The floor is slippery. 要小心。地板很滑。

5. Is your new car blue or red?
   你的新車是藍色還是紅色的？

【註】***over there*** 在那裡　　vacation〔ve'keʃən〕*n.* 假期
careful〔'kɛrfəl〕*adj.* 小心的　　floor〔flor〕*n.* 地板
slippery〔'slɪpərɪ〕*adj.* 滑的

II. 朗讀句子與短文

共有五個句子及一篇短文，請先利用一分
鐘的時間閱讀試卷上的句子與短文，然後
在一分鐘內以正常的速度，清楚正確地朗
讀一遍，請開始閱讀。

One : Can I help you to find anything, sir?
我能幫你找東西嗎，先生？

Two : Where did you go last weekend?
你上個週末去哪裡？

Three : We didn't have enough money, so we couldn't buy
tickets for the show.
我們的錢不夠，所以無法買那場表演的票。

Four : John isn't your cousin, is he?
約翰不是你的表哥，是嗎？

Five : Take the third right and you'll see the store on your
left.
在第三個路口右轉，你就會看到那家商店在你的左邊。

【註】 show〔ʃo〕*n.* 秀；表演
cousin〔'kʌzn̩〕*n.* 表（堂）兄弟姊妹
take the third right 在第三個路口右轉
left〔lɛft〕*n.* 左邊

Six   : It's important for kids to exercise. You can start by
       playing games with your child. Teach him or her
       how to bicycle or roller-skate because these are
       good aerobic activities. You could also start a
       neighborhood baseball or soccer team. Finally, set
       a good example by doing active things instead of
       watching television

對孩子來說，運動很重要。一開始，你可以跟你的孩子
玩遊戲。要教他或她如何騎腳踏車或溜冰，因為這些是
很好的有氧活動。你也可以創立一個鄰近地區的棒球或
足球隊。最後，要樹立好的榜樣，做積極的事，而不是
看電視。

【註】 important〔ɪmˋpɔrtn̩t〕*adj.* 重要的
      exercise〔ˋɛksəˌsaɪz〕*v.* 運動
      bicycle〔ˋbaɪsɪkl̩〕*v.* 騎腳踏車
      roller-skate〔ˋroləˌsket〕*v.* 輪式溜冰
      aerobic〔eəˋrobɪk , ɛˋrobɪk〕*adj.* 有氧的
      activity〔ækˋtɪvətɪ〕*n.* 活動   start〔start〕*v.* 創辦
      neighborhood〔ˋnebəˌhʊd〕*n.* 鄰近地區
      soccer〔ˋsakə〕*n.* 足球   team〔tim〕*n.* 隊
      finally〔ˋfaɪnl̩ɪ〕*adv.* 最後   set〔sɛt〕*v.* 樹立
      example〔ɪgˋzæmpl̩〕*n.* 典範；榜樣
      active〔ˋæktɪv〕*adj.* 積極的；主動的
      instead of 而不是

III. 回答問題

共七題。題目不印在試卷上，由耳機播出，
每題播出兩次，兩次之間大約有一到二秒的
間隔。聽完兩次後，請馬上回答。每題回答
時間為 15 秒，請在作答時間內儘量地表達。

1. **Q** : Did you have any trouble getting here this morning?
   你今天早上到這裡有遇到任何困難嗎？

   A1: Unfortunately, I did. There was a big traffic jam this morning. I was really worried that I was going to be late.
   很遺憾的，我有。今天早上塞車很嚴重。我很擔心我會遲到。

   A2: No, not at all. This building was really easy to find. I even got a parking space right out front.
   不，完全沒有。這棟大樓真的很容易找。我甚至就在門外找到停車位。

   【註】 ***have trouble (in) V-ing*** 做…有困難
   　　 unfortunately〔ʌnˋfɔrtʃənɪtlɪ〕*adv.* 不幸地；遺憾地
   　　 traffic jam 交通阻塞　　 worried〔ˋwɝɪd〕*adj.* 擔心的
   　　 not at all 一點也不　　 building〔ˋbɪldɪŋ〕*n.* 大樓
   　　 parking space 停車位　　 right〔raɪt〕*adv.* 恰好；正好
   　　 out front 在門外

2. **Q** : Do you have any plans for your next vacation?
   你下次的假期有任何的計劃嗎？

A1: Yes, I do. I'm going to Canada with my family.
We'll visit our relatives there.

是的，我有。我要和家人去加拿大。我們會拜訪那裡的親
戚。

A2: No, not really. I'd like to travel somewhere, though.
Maybe I'll go to Hong Kong or Japan.

不，沒有。不過我想去某個地方旅行。或許我會去香港或
日本。

【註】 plan〔plæn〕 *n.* 計畫   Canada〔ˈkænədə〕 *n.* 加拿大
relative〔ˈrɛlətɪv〕 *n.* 親戚   ***not really*** 並沒有
somewhere〔ˈsʌm‚hwɛr〕 *adv.* 到某處
though〔ðo〕 *adv.* 不過【置於句尾】
maybe〔ˈmebɪ〕 *adv.* 或許
Hong Kong〔ˈhɑŋ ˈkɑŋ〕 *n.* 香港
Japan〔dʒəˈpæn〕 *n.* 日本

3. **Q** : What kind of weather do you like?

你喜歡哪一種天氣？

A1: I like cool and crisp weather. It makes me feel
energetic. I also get to wear a nice sweater.

我喜歡清新涼爽的天氣。它會使我覺得充滿活力。我也能
穿一件不錯的毛衣。

A2: Believe it or not, I like rainy weather. I like to sit
inside and watch the rain come down. It makes me
feel very peaceful.

信不信由你，我喜歡下雨的天氣。我喜歡坐在室內看雨落
下來。那會使我覺得非常平靜。

【註】kind〔kaɪnd〕n. 種類　weather〔'wɛðɚ〕n. 天氣
cool〔kul〕adj. 涼爽的
crisp〔krɪsp〕adj. 脆的；清新的；涼爽的
energetic〔ˌɛnɚ'dʒɛtɪk〕adj. 充滿活力的
get to V. 得以…　sweater〔'swɛtɚ〕n. 毛衣
believe it or not 信不信由你　rainy〔'renɪ〕adj. 下雨的
inside〔'ɪn'saɪd〕adv. 在室內
come down （雨、雪）落下
peaceful〔'pisfəl〕adj. 平靜的

4. **Q** : How do you spend your time when you are with
friends?
你會如何度過和朋友在一起的時間？

A1: We usually play a game of some kind. We all like
computer games. We also like sports like soccer and
basketball.
我們通常會玩某種遊戲。我們全都很喜歡電腦遊戲。我們
也喜歡像是足球和籃球之類的運動。

A2: My friends and I spend a lot of time talking. We often
get together at one of our houses. Or we go out for a
meal or a drink.
我的朋友和我會花很多時間談話。我們常會在其中一人的
家裡聚會，或是出去吃頓飯或喝杯飲料。

【註】***of some kind*** 某種的　***get together*** 聚在一起
meal〔mil〕n. 一餐　drink〔drɪŋk〕n. 飲料

5. **Q** : Which do you like better, outdoor activities or indoor
ones? 你比較喜歡哪一種，戶外的活動或是室內的活動？

A1: I like outdoor activities. I really like being out in the fresh air. I enjoy swimming, hiking, and all kinds of sports.

我喜歡戶外的活動。我真的很喜歡出去外面,置身於新鮮的空氣中。我喜歡游泳、健行,和各種運動。

A2: I prefer indoor activities. I like to read and listen to music. I also enjoy going to the movies.

我比較喜歡室內的活動。我喜歡閱讀和聽音樂。我也喜歡去看電影。

【註】 outdoor〔'aʊt,dor〕*adj.* 戶外的
indoor〔'ɪn,dor〕*adj.* 室內的　　fresh〔frɛʃ〕*adj.* 新鮮的
hike〔haɪk〕*v.* 健行　　prefer〔prɪ'fɝ〕*v.* 比較喜歡
go to the movies 去看電影

6. **Q** : Have you ever bought something that you later regretted buying? 你曾經買過事後讓你後悔的東西嗎?

A1: Yes, I have. Once I bought a new cell phone. The very next day I saw the same phone at one third of the price I paid.

是的,我有。有一次我買了一支新手機。就在隔天,我看到一樣的手機,售價是我付的價錢的三分之一。

A2 : I regretted buying my first car. It was used and I didn't know much about cars then. It had a lot of things wrong with it, and I ended up spending a lot of money on it.

我後悔買了我的第一輛車。它是二手的,而我那時對車子不是很了解。它有很多問題,我最後為了它花了很多錢。

【註】ever〔ˋɛvə〕adv. 曾經　　later〔ˋletə〕adv. 後來
　　　regret〔rɪˋɡrɛt〕v. 後悔　　once〔wʌns〕adv. 有一次
　　　cell phone 手機　　very〔ˋvɛrɪ〕adv. 正是；就是
　　　at~price 是~價格　　**a third of** 三分之一的
　　　used〔juzd〕adj. 二手的
　　　wrong〔rɔŋ〕adj. 情況不好的；故障的
　　　end up + **V-ing** 最後~　　spend〔spɛnd〕v. 花費

7. **Q**：Your teacher asks you why you are late. What can you say? 你的老師問你為何遲到。你能怎麼說？

　A1：I can say, "I'm so sorry I'm late. I don't have a good excuse. I promise that it won't happen again."
　　　我可以說：「很抱歉，我遲到了。我沒有很好的藉口。我保證這種事不會再發生。」

　A2：I think I'd say, "I'm sorry I'm late. It wasn't my fault. There was a breakdown on the MRT."
　　　我想我會說：「很抱歉，我遲到了。這不是我的錯。捷運故障了。」

　【註】late〔let〕adj. 遲到的　　excuse〔ɪkˋskjus〕n. 藉口
　　　promise〔ˋprɑmɪs〕v. 保證　　fault〔fɔlt〕n. 過錯
　　　breakdown〔ˋbrekˌdaʊn〕n. 故障　　**the MRT** 捷運

* 請將下列自我介紹的句子再唸一遍，請開始。

My seat number is （複試座位號碼後 5 碼）, and my test number is （初試准考證號碼後 5 碼）.

初級英語檢定複試測驗 ⑤ 詳解

寫作能力測驗詳解

第一部份：單句寫作

第 1～5 題：句子改寫

1. There is a butterfly on the flower.

   There ＿＿＿＿＿＿ two ＿＿＿＿＿＿ on the flower.

   > 重點結構：There is/are 的用法
   >
   > 　解　答：<u>There are two butterflies on the flower.</u>
   >
   > 句型分析：There＋be 動詞＋數詞＋名詞＋地方副詞
   >
   > 　說　明：there is/are 表示「有」，後面為單數名詞，用 is，
   > 　　　　　後面為複數名詞，則用 are。本句的句意為：「有
   > 　　　　　兩隻蝴蝶在這朵花上。」butterflies 為複數名詞，
   > 　　　　　故用 are。
   >
   > ＊ butterfly〔ˈbʌtɚˌflaɪ〕n. 蝴蝶

2. Margaret lives in Taipei.

   Margaret ＿＿＿＿＿＿＿＿＿＿ in Taipei since 2001.

   > 重點結構：since 的用法
   >
   > 　解　答：<u>Margaret has lived in Taipei since 2001.</u>
   >
   > 句型分析：主詞＋have/has＋過去分詞＋since＋時間點
   >
   > 　說　明：本句的句意為：「瑪格麗特從 2001 年就一直住在
   > 　　　　　台北。」由 since（自從）可知，須用「現在完成

式」，即「have/has＋過去分詞」，表「從過去
持續到現在的動作或狀態」，因主詞 Margaret 為
第三人稱單數，故用 has lived。

3. Don't forget to close the window.
   Remember —————————————————————————.

　　重點結構：remember 的用法

　　解　　答：<u>Remember to close the window.</u>

　　句型分析：Remember＋不定詞＋受詞

　　說　　明：本題是由 Remember 為首的祈使句，後面須接不
　　　　　　　定詞，表「記得要去～」（動作未完成）。本句的
　　　　　　　句意為：「記得要去關窗。」

　　* forget〔fəˋgɛt〕v. 忘記　　remember〔rɪˋmɛmbɚ〕v. 記得

4. This is my classmate Diane.
   ————————————————————————, Bob and Steve.

　　重點結構：this 和 these 的用法

　　解　　答：<u>These are my classmates, Bob and Steve.</u>

　　句型分析：These＋are＋複數名詞

　　說　　明：this 表示「這個」，後面接單數 be 動詞 is；
　　　　　　　these 表示「這些」，後面接複數 be 動詞 are。
　　　　　　　本句的句意為：「這些是我的同班同學，鮑伯和
　　　　　　　史蒂芬。」

　　* classmate〔ˋklæsˏmet〕n. 同班同學

5. The girls have a car, don't they?

Gary doesn't _____?

重點結構：附加問句的用法

解　答：<u>Gary doesn't have a car, does he?</u>

句型分析：主詞＋否定助動詞＋原形動詞＋,＋助動詞＋人稱
代名詞？

說　明：敘述句為否定，故附加問句須為肯定，依句意為現
在式，且主詞 Gary 為第三人稱單數，故用 does，
又附加問句的主詞須為敘述句主詞的人稱代名詞，
Gary 的人稱代名詞是 he，故寫成 does he?。
本句的句意為：「蓋瑞沒有車，是嗎？」

第 6～10 題：句子合併

6. The girl is crying.

The girl fell down.

The girl who _____ down.

重點結構：關係代名詞的用法

解　答：<u>The girl who is crying fell down.</u>

句型分析：主詞＋形容詞子句＋動詞 片語

說　明：本句的句意為：「那個正在哭的女孩跌倒了。」
關代 who 引導形容詞子句 who is crying，修飾
先行詞 The girl，後面再接動詞片語 fell down。

* *fall down* 跌倒

7. I can't speak French.
   I can't speak Spanish.
   I _____ or _____.

> 重點結構：or 的用法
>
> 解　答：<u>I can't speak French or Spanish.</u>
>
> 句型分析：主詞＋否定助動詞＋原形動詞＋受詞 A ＋ or ＋
> 　　　　　受詞 B
>
> 說　明：or 在此是表「選擇」的對等連接詞，前後須為文
> 　　　　法功能相同的單字、片語或子句，此題的 or 連接
> 　　　　兩個名詞。本句的句意為：「我不會說法文或西
> 　　　　班牙文。」
>
> * French〔frɛntʃ〕*n.* 法文　　Spanish〔'spænɪʃ〕*n.* 西班牙文

8. Mary visits her grandparents.
   Mary's grandparents live in Taichung.
   Mary _____ who _____.

> 重點結構：關係代名詞的用法
>
> 解　答：<u>Mary visits her grandparents who live in</u>
> 　　　　<u>Taichung.</u>
>
> 句型分析：主詞＋動詞＋受詞＋形容詞子句
>
> 說　明：本句的句意為：「瑪麗去探望她住在台中的祖父
> 　　　　母。」關代 who 引導形容詞子句 who live in
> 　　　　Taichung，修飾先行詞 her grandparents。
>
> * grandparents〔'græn,pɛrənts〕*n. pl.* 祖父母

9. I bought some milk on the way home.

I remembered it.

I remembered _____ home.

重點結構：remember 的用法

解　答：<u>I remembered to buy some milk on the way home.</u>

句型分析：主詞＋remember＋不定詞＋受詞＋副詞片語

說　明：本句的句意為：「我記得在回家的路上買些牛奶。」

remember「記得」有兩種寫法：

{ remember＋to V. 記得去做…【動作未完成】
{ remember＋V-ing 記得做過…【動作已完成】

本句是第一種寫法。

* **on the way home** 在回家的路上

10. I have a new bike.

It is yellow.

I _____ bike.

重點結構：形容詞的排序

解　答：<u>I have a new yellow bike.</u>

句型分析：主詞＋動詞＋不定冠詞＋形容詞＋名詞

說　明：本句的句意為：「我有一輛新的黃色的腳踏車。」new（新的）和 yellow（黃色的）都是用來形容 bicycle（腳踏車）的形容詞，當有數個形容詞用來修飾相同名詞時，排列順序大致如下：大小/長短/形狀 → 新舊 → 顏色 → 國籍 → 材料/性質。

第 11～15 題：重組

11. All _____.

    the game / enjoy / the kids / playing / of

    重點結構：enjoy 的用法

      解　答：<u>All of the kids enjoy playing the game.</u>

    句型分析：主詞＋enjoy＋V-ing

    說　明：enjoy 表示「享受；喜歡」，後面須接名詞或動名
           詞。本句的句意爲：「所有的小孩都很喜歡玩這個
           遊戲。」

12. Ethan _____.

    only 14 / this movie / , so / is / cannot / he / see

    重點結構：so 的用法

      解　答：<u>Ethan is only 14, so he cannot see this movie.</u>

    句型分析：主詞＋動詞＋,＋so＋主詞＋動詞

    說　明：連接詞 because 和 so 的比較：

              結果＋because＋原因
              原因＋so＋結果

           原因是「伊森才 14 歲」，結果是「他不能看那部
           電影」，so 前面是原因，後面接結果。

13. Donna _____.

    lie / parents / never / to / her / would

    重點結構：頻率副詞的用法

      解　答：<u>Donna would never lie to her parents.</u>

句型分析：主詞＋助動詞＋頻率副詞＋原形動詞＋介系詞＋
受詞

說　　明：never 爲頻率副詞，須放在主要動詞前或 be 動詞
後，本句的句意爲：「唐娜絕不會對她的父母說
謊。」

* lie〔laɪ〕v. 說謊

14. Peter ＿＿＿＿＿＿＿＿＿＿＿＿＿＿＿＿＿＿＿＿.
that / leaves / the train / took / at 9:00

重點結構：關係代名詞 that 的用法

解　　答：<u>Peter took the train that leaves at 9:00.</u>

句型分析：主詞＋動詞＋受詞＋形容詞子句

說　　明：本句的句意爲：「彼得搭了九點出發的火車。」
主要子句爲 Peter took the train，而 that 引導
形容詞子句，修飾先行詞 the train。

15. Can ＿＿＿＿＿＿＿＿＿＿＿＿＿＿＿＿＿＿＿＿?
me / with / you / box / this / help / heavy

重點結構：help *sb.* with *sth.* 的用法

解　　答：<u>Can you help me with this heavy box?</u>

句型分析：Can＋主格人稱＋動詞＋受格人稱＋with＋受詞？

說　　明：本句的句意爲：「你能幫我搬這個很重的箱子嗎？」

* ***help sb. with sth.*** 幫助某人某事
heavy〔'hɛvɪ〕*adj.* 重的

第二部份：段落寫作

題目： 兔子 Billy 從農場偷了胡蘿蔔。請根據以下的圖片寫一篇約
　　　 50 字的短文。**注意**：未依提示作答者，將予扣分。

Billy the rabbit loved to eat carrots. ***One day***, he went to
Farmer Jones' field. He pulled the carrots from the ground
one after another. As he was leaving with his basket full of
carrots, he was caught by Farmer Jones. The farmer was
very angry. Poor Billy had to plant all of those carrots back
in the ground again.

　　兔子比利很喜歡吃胡蘿蔔。有一天，牠去了農夫瓊斯的田裡。
牠從地上拔出一根又一根的胡蘿蔔。當牠拿著裝滿胡蘿蔔的籃子要
離開時，被農夫瓊斯抓到了。農夫非常生氣。可憐的比利必須把那
些胡蘿蔔全都再種回地上。

rabbit〔ˈræbɪt〕n. 兔子　　　carrot〔ˈkærət〕n. 胡蘿蔔
farmer〔ˈfɑrmɚ〕n. 農夫　　　field〔fild〕n. 田野
pull〔pʊl〕v. 拉；拔　　　ground〔graʊnd〕n. 地面
one after another 一個接一個　　basket〔ˈbæskɪt〕n. 籃子
full〔fʊl〕adj. 充滿的 <of>　　catch〔kætʃ〕v. 捕捉；逮捕
angry〔ˈæŋgrɪ〕adj. 生氣的　　poor〔pʊr〕adj. 可憐的
plant〔plænt〕v. 種植

口說能力測驗詳解

* 請在 15 秒內完成並唸出下列自我介紹的句子，請開始。

My seat number is （複試座位號碼後 5 碼）, and my test number is （初試准考證號碼後 5 碼）.

I. 複誦

共五題。題目不印在試卷上，由耳機播出，每題播出兩次，兩次之間大約有一到二秒的間隔。聽完兩次後，請馬上複誦一次。

1. Are you using that dictionary? 你正在用那本字典嗎？

2. Look out! The traffic light is red.
   小心！交通號誌燈是紅燈。

3. Would you like some coffee or a soft drink?
   你想要一些咖啡或一杯清涼飲料嗎？

4. When will you arrive at the office?
   你何時會到辦公室？

5. Call me as soon as you arrive. 你一抵達就打電話給我。

【註】 dictionary〔ˈdɪkʃənˌɛrɪ〕n. 字典　　*look out* 小心
　　　 traffic light 交通號誌燈；紅綠燈　　*would like* 想要
　　　 soft drink 不含酒精的飲料；清涼飲料
　　　 arrive〔əˈraɪv〕v. 到達 < *at* >　　office〔ˈɔfɪs〕n. 辦公室
　　　 as soon as 一…就～

II. 朗讀句子與短文

共有五個句子及一篇短文，請先利用一分
鐘的時間閱讀試卷上的句子與短文，然後
在一分鐘內以正常的速度，清楚正確地朗
讀一遍，請開始閱讀。

One　：I sent some flowers to my aunt because it was her
　　　　birthday.

　　　　我送了一些花給我的阿姨，因爲那天是她的生日。

Two　：Where did you put the magazine I gave you?

　　　　你把我給你的雜誌放在哪裡？

Three：Has Vincent been to Taipei before?

　　　　文森以前去過台北嗎？

Four　：There is no need to file the papers now.

　　　　現在不需要把這些文件歸檔。

Five　：Pete is the class leader, isn't he?

　　　　彼特是班長，不是嗎？

【註】 aunt〔ænt〕 n. 阿姨；姑姑
　　　 magazine〔͵mægə′zin〕 n. 雜誌
　　　 have been to 去過　　need〔nid〕 n. 需要
　　　 there is no need to V. 不需要…
　　　 file〔faɪl〕 v. 將…歸檔　　papers〔′pepɚz〕 n. pl. 文件
　　　 class leader 班長

Six　：If your dog gets lost, the first thing you should do is tell your neighbors.　Someone may have seen it. They may also be willing to help you search for the dog.　If you still cannot find it, make some fliers to put up in your neighborhood.　Be sure to include a picture of the dog as well as your contact information.

如果你的狗走失了，你第一件應該做的事，就是告訴你的鄰居。有人可能看過牠，他們可能也會願意幫你尋找那隻狗。如果你還是找不到，就做一些傳單，張貼在你家附近的地區。一定要包含那隻狗的照片，以及你的聯絡資訊。

【註】*get lost* 迷路；走失

the first thing one should do is V. 某人所應該做的第一件事，就是…

neighbor〔'nebɚ〕*n.* 鄰居　　willing〔'wɪlɪŋ〕*adj.* 願意的

search for 尋找　　flier〔'flaɪɚ〕*n.* 傳單

put up 張貼　　neighborhood〔'nebɚ,hʊd〕*n.* 鄰近地區

be sure to V. 一定要～　　include〔ɪn'klud〕*v.* 包括

as well as 以及　　contact〔'kɑntækt〕*adj.* 聯繫用的

information〔,ɪnfɚ'meʃən〕*n.* 資訊

III. 回答問題

共七題。題目不印在試卷上，由耳機播出，
每題播出兩次，兩次之間大約有一到二秒的
間隔。聽完兩次後，請馬上回答。每題回答
時間為 15 秒，請在作答時間內儘量地表達。

1. **Q** : Did you see anything interesting on the way here
today?　你今天來這裡的路上，有看到任何有趣的事嗎？

A1: Well, I saw that there is a big sale at the department
store.　That's interesting to me because I like to go
shopping.　I think I may go there after this test.
嗯，我看到百貨公司正在大特價。那對我來說很有趣，因
為我喜歡購物。我想這場測驗結束後，我可能會去那裡。

A2: I sure did!　I saw someone driving an antique car.　It
looked great, and I think the owner must be really
proud of it.
我的確有！我看到有人開著一輛古董車。它看起來很棒，
我覺得車主一定很自豪。

【註】 interesting (ˈɪntrɪstɪŋ) *adj.* 有趣的
on the way here 在來這裡的途中
sale (sel) *n.* 特價；拍賣　　***department store*** 百貨公司
sure (ʃur) *adv.* 的確；當然
antique (ænˈtik) *adj.* 古董的
great (gret) *adj.* 很棒的　　owner (ˈonɚ) *n.* 擁有者
really (ˈriəlɪ) *adv.* 真地；非常 (= *very*)
proud (praud) *adj.* 驕傲的；自豪的

2. **Q** : Are you usually busy on the weekends?
你週末通常都很忙碌嗎？

A1: No, not usually.　I never do work on the weekend.　I think it's important to relax.

不，通常不會。我從不在週末工作。我認爲放鬆是很重要的。

A2: I sure am!　I always have a lot of housework to do.　I also go out with friends on Saturday, and I go to church on Sunday.

我的確是！我總是有很多家事要做。我在星期六也會和朋友出去，而且星期天我會去上教堂。

【註】 usually ('juʒʊəlɪ) *adv.* 通常
on the weekends 在週末 (= *on weekends* = *on the weekend*)　　relax (rɪ'læks) *v.* 放鬆
housework ('haʊs,wɝk) *n.* 家事
church (tʃɝtʃ) *n.* 教堂　　*go to church* 上教堂

3. **Q** : What do you like to do on a rainy day?
你喜歡在下雨天做什麼？

A1: I like to rent a DVD and stay in.　Sometimes I watch a movie I missed at the theater.　Other times I watch an old favorite.

我喜歡租一片 DVD 並待在家裡。有時候我會看沒去電影院看的電影。其他時候，我會看一部我最喜愛的老電影。

A2: I usually play computer games.　Rain is a perfect excuse to stay in and do that.　Sometimes I wish it would rain more often!

我通常會玩電腦遊戲。下雨是個完美的藉口，能待在家裡打電玩。有時候我真希望能更常下雨！

【註】 rent (rɛnt) *v.* 租

DVD *n.* 數位影音光碟 (= *digital video disk*)
stay in 待在家；不出門
sometimes…other times 有時…有時
miss〔mɪs〕*v.* 錯過　　theater〔'θiətɚ〕*n.* 電影院
favorite〔'fevərɪt〕*n.* 最喜愛的人或物
perfect〔'pɝfɪkt〕*adj.* 完美的
excuse〔ɪk'skjus〕*n.* 藉口　　wish〔wɪʃ〕*v.* 希望

4. **Q** : Do you have any special skills or talents, such as
painting or singing?
你有任何特別的技巧或才能嗎，像是畫畫或唱歌？

A1: Well, I'm pretty good at playing the violin. I started
taking lessons when I was six. Now I play in my
school orchestra.
嗯，我很擅長拉小提琴。我六歲開始上小提琴課。現在我
在學校的管絃樂團演奏。

A2: My friends say I'm a good singer. They often ask me
to sing at parties. I don't know if I'm really that good,
but I like doing it.
我的朋友說我很會唱歌。他們常常要求我在派對上唱歌。
我不知道我是不是真的唱得那麼好，但我很喜歡唱歌。

【註】special〔'spɛʃəl〕*adj.* 特別的　　skill〔skɪl〕*n.* 技巧
talent〔'tælənt〕*n.* 才能　　***such as*** 像是
painting〔'pentɪŋ〕*n.* 繪畫　　***be good at*** 擅長
pretty〔'prɪtɪ〕*adv.* 相當　　violin〔͵vaɪə'lɪn〕*n.* 小提琴
play the violin 拉小提琴　　***take lessons*** 上課
orchestra〔'ɔrkɪstrə〕*n.* 管絃樂團

5. **Q** : Which do you like better, writing e-mails or talking on
the phone? 你比較喜歡哪一個，寫電子郵件還是講電話？

A1: I like talking on the phone much better. It's a lot more fun to hear my friend's voice. Also, I can get an answer right away.

我比較喜歡講電話。能聽到朋友的聲音有趣很多。此外，我能立刻得到回答。

A2: I prefer to send e-mails. It gives me more time to think about what I want to say. It's a lot cheaper, too!

比較喜歡寄電子郵件。這能給我較多的時間，思考我想要說的話。而且也便宜很多！

【註】 e-mail〔'i,mel〕 *n.* 電子郵件
talk on the phone 講電話　　*like ~ better* 比較喜歡～
fun〔fʌn〕 *adj.* 有趣的　　voice〔vɔɪs〕 *n.* 聲音
right away 立刻　　prefer〔prɪ'fɝ〕 *v.* 比較喜歡
cheap〔tʃip〕 *adj.* 便宜的

6. **Q**：Have you ever been to a surprise party?

你曾經參加過驚喜派對嗎？

A1：Yes, I went to one for my friend last year. It was his birthday. He didn't suspect a thing and was really surprised.

有，我去年參加過一個為我朋友辦的。那天是他的生日。他一點都沒有懷疑，所以非常驚訝。

A2：In fact, my friends gave me a surprise party on my birthday. I had no idea what they were planning. I was really touched by their thoughtfulness.

事實上，我的朋友們在我生日那天，幫我辦了一個驚喜派對。我不知道他們的計畫。對於他們的體貼，我實在很感動。

【註】surprise〔sə'praɪz〕n. 驚訝 v. 使驚訝
not…a thing 什麼也沒有…
suspect〔sə'spɛkt〕v. 懷疑 in fact 事實上
have no idea 不知道 touch〔tʌtʃ〕v. 使感動
thoughtfulness〔'θɔtfəlnɪs〕n. 體貼

7. **Q** : Your friend has a bad cold. What can you say to him?
你的朋友得了重感冒。你可以對他說什麼？

A1: I'd say, "You should take care of yourself. Have you been to see a doctor? Is there anything I can do for you?"
我會說：「你應該要照顧你自己。你有去看醫生了嗎？有什麼我能為你做的？」

A2: I'd probably say, "I'm sorry you're not feeling well. Try to take it easy for a few days. I hope you feel better soon."
我可能會說：「你覺得不舒服我很難過。試著放鬆幾天。我希望你能很快就好起來。」

【註】cold〔kold〕n. 感冒 have a bad cold 得了重感冒
take care of 照顧 probably〔'prɑbəblɪ〕adv. 可能
well〔wɛl〕adj. 健康的；安好的 take it easy 放輕鬆
hope〔hop〕v. 希望 soon〔sun〕adv. 很快

＊請將下列自我介紹的句子再唸一遍，請開始。

My seat number is (複試座位號碼後5碼) , and my test number is (初試准考證號碼後5碼) .

初級英語檢定複試測驗⑥詳解

寫作能力測驗詳解

第一部份：單句寫作

第1～5題：句子改寫

1. Arthur ate a sandwich for lunch.

   Did ＿＿＿＿＿＿＿＿＿＿＿＿＿＿ a sandwich for lunch?

   > **重點結構：**直述句改爲疑問句
   >
   > **解　答：**Did Arthur eat a sandwich for lunch?
   >
   > **句型分析：**助動詞＋主詞＋原形動詞＋受詞＋介系詞片語
   >
   > **説　明：**直述句改爲疑問句，依句意爲過去式，故句首的助
   > 動詞用 Did，接主詞 Arthur 後，再接原形動詞
   > eat。本句的句意爲：「亞瑟吃三明治當午餐嗎？」
   >
   > * sandwich〔'sændwɪtʃ〕*n.* 三明治

2. Betty enjoys playing the piano.

   Betty likes to ＿＿＿＿＿＿＿＿＿＿＿＿＿＿＿＿＿.

   > **重點結構：**like 的用法
   >
   > **解　答：**Betty likes to play the piano.
   >
   > **句型分析：**主詞＋like＋不定詞＋受詞
   >
   > **説　明：**enjoy（喜歡）須接名詞或動名詞，而 like（喜歡）
   > 則須接不定詞，故寫成 likes to play the piano。
   > 本句的句意爲：「貝蒂喜歡彈鋼琴。」
   >
   > * piano〔pɪ'æno〕*n.* 鋼琴　　***play the piano*** 彈鋼琴

3. My brother gave me a book.

   _____ to me.

   > 重點結構：give 的用法
   >
   > 解　答：<u>My brother gave a book to me.</u>
   >
   > 句型分析：主詞＋give＋直接受詞（物）＋to＋間接受詞（人）
   >
   > 説　明：授與動詞 give 的寫法有兩種：
   > $$\begin{cases} \text{give＋間接受詞（人）＋直接受詞（物）} \\ \text{give＋直接受詞（物）＋to＋間接受詞（人）} \end{cases}$$
   > 本句爲第二種寫法。

4. The children were skating in the park yesterday.

   The children _____ every day.

   > 重點結構：過去進行式改爲現在簡單式
   >
   > 解　答：<u>The children skate in the park every day.</u>
   >
   > 句型分析：主詞＋動詞＋地方副詞＋時間副詞
   >
   > 説　明：由 every day（每天）可知，本句爲現在簡單式，
   > 故將過去進行式 were skating 改成現在簡單式
   > skate。本句的句意爲：「那些小孩每天在公園裡
   > 溜冰。」
   >
   > ＊ skate〔sket〕v. 溜冰

5. No, I couldn't hear the music before.

   No, I _____ hear the music now.

   > 重點結構：過去式的回答改爲現在式的回答
   >
   > 解　答：<u>No, I can't hear the music now.</u>

句型分析：No +，+ 主詞 + 否定助動詞 + 原形動詞 + 受詞 +
　　　　　時間副詞

　說　　明：由 now 可知，時態為現在式，故將過去式助動詞否
　　　　　定 couldn't 改為現在式助動詞否定 can't。本句的
　　　　　句意為：「不，我現在聽不到音樂。」

第 6～10 題：句子合併

6. Paula's mother will give her a present.

　Paula gets an A on the test.

　If _____ present.

　重點結構：If 的用法

　　解　答：If Paula gets an A on the test, her mother will
　　　　　give her a present.

　句型分析：If + 主詞 + 動詞 + 受詞 + 介系詞片語 +，+ 主詞 +
　　　　　助動詞 + 原形動詞 + 間接受詞 + 直接受詞

　　說　明：本句的句意為：「如果寶拉考試得到甲等，她的媽
　　　　　媽就會給她一個禮物。」If 引導表條件的副詞子句，
　　　　　用現在式代替未來式，為了避免重複，將 Paula's
　　　　　mother 改為 her mother。

　　* present〔'prɛznt〕n. 禮物　　A〔e〕n. 甲等

7. Please hand me the dictionary.

　The dictionary is on the desk.

　Please _____ desk.

　重點結構：關代 which/that 的用法

解　答：<u>Please hand me the dictionary (that/which is)</u>
　　　　<u>on the desk.</u>

句型分析：Please＋原形動詞＋間接受詞（人）＋直接受詞
　　　　　（物）＋介系詞片語

說　明：本句的句意為：「請把書桌上的字典拿給我。」
　　　　用關代 that 或 which 引導形容詞子句，修飾先行
　　　　詞 the dictionary，也可省略關代和 be 動詞，用
　　　　介系詞片語 on the desk 修飾 the dictionary。

＊ hand〔hænd〕v. 拿給　　***hand sb. sth.*** 把某物拿給某人

8. Nancy has a computer and a cell phone.
　 The cell phone is new.
　 Nancy _____ cell phone.

重點結構：形容詞修飾名詞

解　答：<u>Nancy has a computer and a new cell phone.</u>

句型分析：主詞＋動詞＋名詞 A＋and＋形容詞＋名詞 B

說　明：本句的句意為：「南西有一台電腦和一支新的手
　　　　機。」形容詞 new 修飾名詞 cell phone。

＊ computer〔kəm'pjutɚ〕n. 電腦　　***cell phone*** 手機

9. We can eat our chicken here.
　 We can take our chicken home.
　 We can eat _____ home.

重點結構：or 的用法

解　答：<u>We can eat our chicken here or take it home.</u>

句型分析：主詞＋助動詞＋原形動詞＋受詞＋地方副詞＋or＋
原形動詞＋受詞＋地方副詞

說　明：表「選擇」的連接詞 or 連接兩個動詞片語 eat our
chicken here 和 take it home。本句的句意為：
「我們可以在這裡吃我們的雞肉，或把它帶回家。」

10. The man is standing by the door.

The man is our teacher.

The man who ＿＿＿＿＿＿＿＿＿＿＿＿＿＿＿＿＿＿ teacher.

重點結構：關代 who 的用法

解　答：The man who is standing by the door is our
teacher.

句型分析：主詞＋形容詞子句＋be 動詞＋主詞補語

說　明：本句的句意為：「站在門旁的那個男人是我們的老
師。」關代 who 引導形容詞子句，修飾先行詞 The
man。

第 11～15 題：重組

11. Here ＿＿＿＿＿＿＿＿＿＿＿＿＿＿＿＿＿＿＿＿＿＿＿.

you / is / lent / the book / me

重點結構：here 的用法

解　答：Here is the book you lent me.

句型分析：Here＋be 動詞＋主詞＋(關代)＋主詞＋動詞＋
受詞

說　明：地方副詞 Here (在這裡) 置於句首時，主詞和 be

動詞須倒裝，寫成：Here is the book，又關代
which 或 that 引導形容詞子句，修飾先行詞 the
book，在子句中，關代如當受詞，可省略。本句
的句意爲：「這就是你借我的那本書。」

* lend〔lɛnd〕v. 借（出）

12. The _____.
was on sale, / coat / I / so / decided / it / to buy

重點結構：so 的用法

解　答：The coat was on sale, so I decided to buy it.

句型分析：主詞＋be 動詞＋介系詞片語＋, ＋so＋主詞＋動詞
＋不定詞＋受詞

説　明：本句的句意爲：「那件外套在特價，所以我決定要
買它。」so 引導表結果的副詞子句，修飾 be 動詞
was。

* *on sale* 特價；拍賣　　decide〔dɪ'saɪd〕v. 決定

13. What _____?
did / you / last night / time / arrive / home

重點結構：What time 的用法

解　答：What time did you arrive home last night?

句型分析：What time＋助動詞＋主詞＋原形動詞＋地方副詞
＋時間副詞？

説　明：這句的句意爲：「你昨晚何時到家？」疑問副詞
What time（什麼時候）（＝*When*）置於句首，

依句意爲過去式，故先接過去式助動詞 did，再接
主詞 you，再加原形動詞 arrive。

14. Please _____.

how to / the machine / tell / operate / me

重點結構：tell 的用法

解　答：<u>Please tell me how to operate the machine.</u>

句型分析：Please＋tell＋間接受詞＋直接受詞（名詞片語）

說　明：本句的句意爲：「請告訴我如何操作這個機器。」
tell *sb. sth.*「告訴某人某事」，接人（me）之後，
須接名詞片語，可用「疑問詞＋不定詞＋受詞」的
形式，即 how to operate the machine。

* operate〔'ɑpə,ret〕*v.* 操作　　machine〔mə'ʃin〕*n.* 機器

15. Mr. and Mrs. _____.

eat / Williams / usually / at 6:00 / dinner

重點結構：頻率副詞 usually 的用法

解　答：<u>Mr. and Mrs. Williams usually eat dinner at
6:00.</u>

句型分析：主詞＋頻率副詞＋一般動詞＋受詞＋時間副詞

說　明：本句的句意爲：「威廉斯夫婦通常在六點吃晚餐。」
主詞是 Mr. and Mrs. Williams（威廉斯夫婦），
usually（通常）是頻率副詞，須置於一般動詞前，
be 動詞後，故寫成 usually eat dinner at 6:00。

* usually〔'juʒʊəlɪ〕*adv.* 通常

第二部份：段落寫作

題目：Steve 很用力地把球打出去。請根據以下的圖片寫一篇約 50
　　　字的短文。**注意**：未依提示作答者，將予扣分。

　　Steve and his friends were playing baseball. Steve could
not run fast, but he could hit the ball hard. When he hit it,
the ball flew across the field. He thought it would be a home
run, so he walked casually around the bases. ***But then*** the
ball hit the kennel of a mean dog. The dog chased Steve,
and Steve found that he could run very fast after all.

　　史蒂夫和他的朋友正在打棒球。史蒂夫無法跑得很快，但他能
用力打球。當他打中球時，球飛越了球場。他認為那將會是全壘
打，所以他漫不經心的走在各壘之間。但是後來那顆球打到了一隻
兇惡的狗的狗屋。那隻狗追著史蒂夫，而史蒂夫發現，他終究還是
可以跑得非常快的。

hit〔hɪt〕v. 打擊　　hard〔hɑrd〕adv. 用力地
fly〔flaɪ〕n. 飛【三態變化：fly-flew-flown】
field〔fild〕n.（棒球）球場　　***home run*** 全壘打
casually〔ˈkæʒʊəlɪ〕adv. 漫不經心地
around〔əˈraʊnd〕prep. 在…到處　　base〔bes〕n. 壘
kennel〔ˈkɛnḷ〕n. 狗舍　　mean〔min〕adj. 兇惡的
chase〔tʃes〕v. 追　　***after all*** 畢竟；終究

口說能力測驗詳解

＊請在 15 秒內完成並唸出下列自我介紹的句子，請開始。

My seat number is （複試座位號碼後 5 碼）, and my test number is （初試准考證號碼後 5 碼）.

I. 複誦

共五題。題目不印在試卷上，由耳機播出，每題播出兩次，兩次之間大約有一到二秒的間隔。聽完兩次後，請馬上複誦一次。

1. I'll be right with you. 馬上來。

2. Is this your pen or mine?
   這是你的筆還是我的？

3. Who were you talking to?
   你正在跟誰說話？

4. No, thanks. I don't want one.
   不了，謝謝。我不想要。

5. Do you need some help with that?
   那個你需要人幫忙嗎？

【註】 right〔raɪt〕*adv.* 立刻；馬上
I'll be right with you. 馬上來。

II. 朗讀句子與短文

共有五個句子及一篇短文，請先利用一分鐘的時間閱讀試卷上的句子與短文，然後在一分鐘內以正常的速度，清楚正確地朗讀一遍，請開始閱讀。

One　：　We can go to the zoo tomorrow, or we could wait until Sunday.

我們可以明天去動物園，或是等到星期天。

Two　：　Is this a picture of your family?

這是你家人的照片嗎？

Three：　You can give me a ride to the station, can't you?

你能載我去車站，不能嗎？

Four　：　How often do you talk to Jason?

你和傑森多久說一次話？

Five　：　Wait. I'll help you carry those boxes.

等一下。我會幫你搬那些箱子。

【註】 zoo〔zu〕n. 動物園
give sb. a ride 開車載某人；讓某人搭便車
carry〔ˈkærɪ〕v. 搬運

Six　　：　No matter how busy you are, you can get more done if you manage your time well. Try making a schedule or to-do list for important tasks. Plan to do the most difficult things at the time of day when you are most alert. Also, learn to say no to others if you don't have time to do them a favor.

　　　　無論你有多忙，如果能好好管理時間，你就能完成更多事。試著為重要的工作制定時間表或計劃表。要計劃在你一天之中最警覺的時刻，做最困難的事。而且要學會拒絕別人，如果你沒時間幫他們的忙的話。

【註】 *no matter* 無論　　manage〔'mænɪdʒ〕*v.* 管理
schedule〔'skɛdʒul〕*n.* 時間表　　list〔lɪst〕*n.* 名單；清單
to-do list 執行表；計劃表　　alert〔ə'lɝt〕*adj.* 警覺的
say no to 拒絕　　favor〔'fevə〕*n.* 恩惠
do sb. a favor 幫某人的忙

III. 回答問題

共七題。題目不印在試卷上，由耳機播出，每題播出兩次，兩次之間大約有一到二秒的間隔。聽完兩次後，請馬上回答。每題回答時間為 15 秒，請在作答時間內儘量地表達。

1. **Q**：How long did it take you to get here today?
　　你今天到這裡花多久的時間？

A1: It took me about half an hour. I don't live too far
away. I was able to take a bus directly from my
neighborhood.
花了我大約一個半小時。我不是住得很遠。我可以在我家
附近直接搭公車。

A2: Quite a while, actually. I had to take a train and then
change to a bus. But I allowed myself plenty of time,
so I wasn't worried.
事實上，相當久。我必須搭火車，然後換公車。但是我讓
自己預留很多時間，所以我不擔心。

【註】 take〔tek〕v. 花費   ***be able to V***. 能夠…
directly〔dəˈrɛktlɪ〕adv. 直接地
neighborhood〔ˈnebɚˌhud〕n. 鄰近地區
quite a while 好一陣子；很久
actually〔ˈæktʃuəlɪ〕adv. 事實上
change〔tʃendʒ〕v. 換乘   allow〔əˈlau〕v. 給予
plenty of 很多的   worried〔ˈwɝɪd〕adj. 擔心的

2. **Q** : How do you usually spend your birthday?
你通常會如何過生日？

A1: I always celebrate it with my family. My mom makes
a cake and a nice dinner. My family sing Happy
Birthday to me, and they give me some presents, too.
我總是和家人一起慶祝。我媽媽會做一個蛋糕和一頓豐盛
的晚餐。我的家人會對我唱生日快樂歌，也會給我一些禮
物。

A2: I never know how I'm going to spend my next birthday. That's because I always try something new on my birthday. It's kind of a tradition for me.

我從不知道我會如何過下一個生日。那是因為我生日時總是會嘗試新事物。那對我來說有點像是一種傳統。

【註】 spend〔spɛnd〕v. 度過　　celebrate〔'sɛlə,bret〕v. 慶祝
present〔'prɛznt〕n. 禮物　　try〔traɪ〕v. 嘗試
kind of 有點；可以說　　tradition〔trə'dɪʃən〕n. 傳統

3. **Q**：Do you like rainy days? Why or why not?

你喜歡下雨天嗎？為什麼喜歡，或為什麼不喜歡？

A1: No, I don't like it when it rains. The rain makes it inconvenient to go out. I don't like being stuck indoors.

不，我不喜歡下雨天。下雨使得出門很不方便。我不喜歡被困在室內。

A2: I like rainy days. The rain makes the city seem quieter. It's also a lot fresher and greener after it stops.

我喜歡下雨天。雨讓城市似乎更安靜了。雨停了之後，也變得更清新和更翠綠。

【註】 rainy〔'renɪ〕adj. 下雨的
inconvenient〔,ɪnkən'vinjənt〕adj. 不方便的
stuck〔stʌk〕adj. 困住的
indoors〔'ɪn'dors〕adv. 在室內
quiet〔'kwaɪət〕adj. 安靜的　　seem〔sim〕v. 似乎
fresh〔frɛʃ〕adj. 新鮮的；（空氣）清新的
green〔grin〕adj. 綠油油的

4. **Q** : How do you spend your time when you are alone?
   當你獨自一人時,會如何打發時間?

   A1: I usually read a book or listen to music. I especially
   like to read when no one else is around. It's a lot
   easier to concentrate.
   我通常會看書或聽音樂。當沒有別人在身邊時,我尤其喜
   歡閱讀。這樣比較容易專心。

   A2: I don't really like to be alone. So I often go online
   and chat with someone. If I'm really feeling lonely,
   I'll pick up the phone and call a friend.
   我並不喜歡獨處,所以我常上網和人聊天。如果我真得覺
   得寂寞,我會拿起電話,打給朋友。

   【註】 alone〔ə'lon〕*adj.* 獨自的
   especially〔ə'spɛʃəlɪ〕*adv.* 尤其
   else〔ɛls〕*adj.* 其他的;別的
   around〔ə'raʊnd〕*adv.* 在附近
   concentrate〔'kɑnsṇ,tret〕*v.* 專心   ***go online*** 上網
   chat〔tʃæt〕*v.* 聊天   lonely〔'lonlɪ〕*adj.* 寂寞的
   pick up 拿起   call〔kɔl〕*v.* 打電話給

5. **Q** : Which do you like better, dogs or cats? Why?
   你比較喜歡哪一個,狗還是貓?為什麼?

   A1: I like dogs better. They're much more social than cats.
   I really like playing with mine and taking it for a walk.
   我比較喜歡狗。牠們比貓要合群多了。我真的很喜歡和我
   的狗玩,並帶牠去散步。

A2: I prefer cats. They're really cute and easy to care for. I think they're the perfect pet.

我比較喜歡貓。牠們眞的很可愛，而且容易照顧。我認爲牠們是完美的寵物。

【註】 *like…better* 比較喜歡…

social〔'soʃəl〕*adj.* 群居的；喜歡交際的；合群的

walk〔wɔk〕*n.* 散步　　prefer〔prɪ'fɜ〕*v.* 比較喜歡

cute〔kjut〕*adj.* 可愛的　　*care for* 照顧

perfect〔'pɜfɪkt〕*adj.* 完美的　　pet〔pɛt〕*n.* 寵物

6. **Q**：Have you ever met a foreign tourist in your country?

你曾經在你的國家遇過外國遊客嗎？

A1: Once I met some tourists from Japan. They asked me how to get to a museum. I told them, and I also recommended a good restaurant where they could eat lunch.

有一次我遇見了一些來自日本的遊客。他們問我如何去博物館。我告訴了他們，並且也推薦一間他們可以吃午餐的好餐廳。

A2: No, I never have. I would like to meet a foreign visitor, though. I'd like to show off my city and country.

不，我從未遇見過。不過，我很想遇見外國遊客。我想要炫耀我的城市和國家。

【註】 ever〔'ɛvɚ〕*adv.* 曾經　　foreign〔'fɔrɪn〕*adj.* 外國的

tourist〔'turɪst〕*n.* 遊客　　country〔'kʌntrɪ〕*n.* 國家

once〔wʌns〕*adv.* 有一次　　Japan〔dʒə'pæn〕*n.* 日本

museum〔mju'ziəm〕*n.* 博物館

recommend〔,rɛkə'mɛnd〕v. 推薦
restaurant〔'rɛstərənt〕n. 餐廳　　***show off*** 炫耀

7. **Q**：Your friend is wearing an ugly shirt and asks you what you think.　What can you say?
你的朋友正穿著一件很醜的襯衫，並且問你的看法。你可以說什麼？

A1：I think I should tell the truth in a nice way.　I'd say, "That shirt doesn't really suit you.　I think you'd look better in a different color."
我認為我應該用比較好的方式說實話。我會說：「那件襯衫不是很適合你。我想你穿另一個顏色會比較好看。」

A2：I wouldn't want to hurt my friend's feelings.　I'd say, "Your shirt is really unusual.　It's a very different design."
我不想傷害朋友的感情。我會說：「你的襯衫真的很不尋常。它是一種非常特別的設計。」

【註】ugly〔'ʌglɪ〕adj. 醜的　　truth〔truθ〕n. 實話
nice〔naɪs〕adj. 好的　　way〔we〕n. 方式
suit〔sut〕v. 適合　　in〔ɪn〕prep. 穿著
hurt〔hɜt〕v. 傷害　　feelings〔'filɪŋz〕n. pl. 感情
unusual〔ʌn'juʒʊəl〕adj. 不尋常的
different〔'dɪfrənt〕adj. 不同的
design〔dɪ'zaɪn〕n. 設計

＊請將下列自我介紹的句子再唸一遍，請開始。

My seat number is （複試座位號碼後 5 碼）, and my test number is （初試准考證號碼後 5 碼）.

初級英語檢定複試測驗 ⑦ 詳解

寫作能力測驗詳解

第一部份：單句寫作

第 1～5 題：句子改寫

1. Walter just arrived at the office.

   Walter usually ＿＿＿＿＿＿＿＿＿＿ at the office at 9:00.

   > **重點結構**：過去式改爲現在式
   >
   > **解　答**：<u>Walter usually arrives at the office at 9:00.</u>
   >
   > **句型分析**：主詞＋頻率副詞＋一般動詞＋地方副詞＋時間副詞
   >
   > **説　明**：過去式改爲現在式，副詞由 just（剛剛）改爲
   > usually（通常），動詞則由 arrived 改爲 arrives。
   > 本句的句意爲：「華特通常在九點抵達辦公室。」

2. My sister's hat is blue.

   My sisters' ＿＿＿＿＿＿＿＿＿＿ blue.

   > **重點結構**：單數名詞改爲複數名詞
   >
   > **解　答**：<u>My sisters' hats are blue.</u>
   >
   > **句型分析**：主詞＋be 動詞＋形容詞
   >
   > **説　明**：原句主詞 My sister's hat 爲單數，故 be 動詞用
   > is。若主詞改爲 My sisters' hats 則爲複數，be
   > 動詞須改成 are。

3. I am going to see a movie tomorrow.

I _____ a movie yesterday.

重點結構：未來式改為過去式

解　答：<u>I went to see a movie yesterday.</u>

句型分析：主詞＋過去式動詞＋受詞＋時間副詞

說　明：原句時間副詞為 tomorrow，故動詞用 be going to see（將要去看）表未來式。時間點改為 yesterday，則動詞須改成過去式 went to see。

4. Where is my pencil?

Do you know _____?

重點結構：間接問句的用法

解　答：<u>Do you know where my pencil is?</u>

句型分析：Do you know＋疑問詞＋主詞＋動詞？

說　明：Do you know 後面須接受詞，故疑問句 Where is my pencil? 須改為間接問句，當 know 的受詞，即「疑問詞＋主詞＋動詞」的形式。本句的句意為：「你知道我的鉛筆在哪裡嗎？」

5. He is the man that lives next door.

They are the children _____.

重點結構：單數主詞改為複數主詞

解　答：<u>They are the children that live next door.</u>

句型分析：主詞＋be 動詞＋補語＋that＋動詞＋地方副詞

說　明：本句的句意為：「他們是住在隔壁的孩子。」

that 在此爲關係代名詞，代替先行詞 the children，引導形容詞子句，故主要子句 They are the children 放在 that 之前。因爲先行詞 the children 爲複數，故形容詞子句裡的動詞 live 不加 s。

* **next door** 在隔壁

第 6～10 題：句子合併

6. Jack lives in Taipei.

Jack moved to Taipei in 2001.

Jack ＿＿＿＿＿＿＿＿＿＿＿＿＿＿＿＿＿ since 2001.

　　重點結構：since 的用法

　　解　答：<u>Jack has lived in Taipei since 2001.</u>

　　句型分析：主詞＋have/has＋過去分詞＋since＋時間點

　　説　明：由 since 2001 可知，須用「現在完成式」（have/has＋過去分詞），表「從過去持續到現在的動作或狀態」，故用 has lived。本句的句意爲：「傑克從 2001 年以來，就一直住在台北。」

　　* move〔muv〕*v.* 搬家

7. Mark wants to buy a book.

He wants an interesting book.

Mark ＿＿＿＿＿＿＿＿＿＿＿＿＿＿＿＿＿ book.

　　重點結構：形容詞修飾名詞

　　解　答：<u>Mark wants to buy an interesting book.</u>

句型分析：主詞＋動詞＋不定詞＋不定冠詞＋形容詞＋名詞

說　明：want（想要）後面須接不定詞，又形容詞須放在名
詞前，修飾名詞，故 interesting 放在 book 前面。
本句的句意為：「馬克想要買一本有趣的書。」

* interesting〔'ɪntrɪstɪŋ〕adj. 有趣的

8. Here are the magazines.
You asked me for them.
Here ＿＿＿＿＿＿＿＿ that ＿＿＿＿＿＿＿＿＿＿＿＿.

重點結構：that 的用法

解　答：<u>Here are the magazines that you asked me for.</u>

句型分析：Here＋be 動詞＋主詞＋that＋主詞＋動詞＋受詞

說　明：本句的句意為：「這些是你向我要的雜誌。」關係
代名詞 that 引導形容詞子句，修飾先行詞 the
magazines。

* magazine〔ˌmæg'zin〕n. 雜誌　　***ask for*** 要求

9. Jack went to the movie.
He had already seen it.
Jack ＿＿＿＿＿＿＿＿ even though ＿＿＿＿＿＿＿＿＿.

重點結構：even though 的用法

解　答：<u>Jack went to the movie even though he had</u>
<u>already seen it.</u>

句型分析：主詞＋動詞＋介系詞＋受詞＋even though＋主詞
＋副詞＋動詞＋受詞

說　明：本句的句意爲：「傑克去看那部電影，即使他已經
　　　　看過了。」連接詞 even though（即使）引導副詞
　　　　子句，修飾主要動詞 went。

10. Is that the phone?

You bought it yesterday.

Is ＿＿＿＿＿＿＿＿＿＿＿＿＿＿＿＿＿＿＿ yesterday?

重點結構：that 引導形容詞子句

解　答：<u>Is that the phone (that) you bought yesterday?</u>

句型分析：Is＋主詞＋補語＋(that)＋主詞＋動詞＋時間副詞？

說　明：第一個 that 是指示代名詞，第二個 that 爲關係代名
　　　　詞，代替先行詞 the phone，引導形容詞子句，而
　　　　當關代爲受詞時，可省略。本句的句意爲：「那是
　　　　你昨天買的電話嗎？」

　* phone〔fon〕*n.* 電話

第 11～15 題：重組

11. Henry ＿＿＿＿＿＿＿＿＿＿＿＿＿＿＿＿＿＿.

swim / at / to / likes / the beach

重點結構：like 的用法

解　答：<u>Henry likes to swim at the beach.</u>

句型分析：主詞＋動詞＋不定詞＋地方副詞

說　明：like 表示「喜歡」，後面可接不定詞或動名詞。
　　　　本句的句意爲：「亨利喜歡在海邊游泳。」

　* beach〔bitʃ〕*n.* 海灘；海邊

12. We _____.
    saw / funny movies, / like / so / a comedy / we

    重點結構：so 的用法

      解　答：<u>We like funny movies, so we saw a comedy.</u>

    句型分析：主詞＋動詞＋受詞＋, ＋so＋主詞＋動詞＋受詞

      說　明：連接詞 because 和 so 的比較：

$$\begin{cases} 結果＋because＋原因 \\ 原因＋so＋結果 \end{cases}$$

          原因是「我們喜歡好笑的電影」，結果是「我們去看了一部喜劇」，so 前面放原因，後面放結果。

    ＊ funny〔ˈfʌnɪ〕*adj.* 喜劇　　comedy〔ˈkɑmədɪ〕*n.* 喜劇

13. The girls _____.
    take / lunch / usually / after / a nap

    重點結構：頻率副詞的用法

      解　答：<u>The girls usually take a nap after lunch.</u>

    句型分析：主詞＋頻率副詞＋動詞＋受詞＋時間副詞

      說　明：usually 為頻率副詞，須放在主要動詞前或 be 動詞後，本句的句意為：「這些女孩通常午餐後都會睡午覺。」

    ＊ *take a nap* 小睡；睡午覺

14. Do _____?
    walk / you / to school / always

    重點結構：疑問句的基本結構

解　答：<u>Do you always walk to school?</u>

句型分析：Do + 主詞 + 頻率副詞 + 動詞 + 介系詞 + 受詞？

説　明：本句的句意為：「你總是走路去上學嗎？」always
表示「總是」，為頻率副詞，須放在主要動詞前或
be 動詞後。

15. I _____.

yesterday / bought / I / the bag / saw / that

重點結構：that 的用法

解　答：<u>I bought the bag that I saw yesterday.</u>

句型分析：主詞 + 動詞 + 受詞（先行詞）+ 關係代名詞（that）
+ 主詞 + 動詞 + 時間點

説　明：that 在此為關係代名詞，代替先行詞 the bag，引導
形容詞子句。本句的句意為：「我買了我昨天看到
的包包。」主要子句 I bought the bag 放在 that 之
前，I saw yesterday 放在 that 之後。

第二部份：段落寫作

題目：　貓追趕老鼠進洞並聽到狗叫聲。請根據以下的圖片寫一篇約
50 字的短文。**注意：**未依提示作答者，將予扣分。

A cat was chasing a mouse. Fortunately, the mouse was able to run into its hole. The mean cat waited outside the hole. Suddenly it heard a dog barking loudly. It was afraid, so it ran away to hide. *Meanwhile*, inside the hole, the mouse was practicing speaking the dog language. The cat had been fooled by the bilingual mouse!

有隻貓正在追一隻老鼠。幸運的是,老鼠能夠跑進牠的洞裡。那隻兇惡的貓在洞的外面等。突然間,牠聽到一隻狗叫得很大聲。牠很害怕,所以就跑去躲起來。同時,那隻在洞裡的老鼠,正在練習說狗的語言。那隻貓被這隻會兩種語言的老鼠騙了!

chase〔tʃes〕v. 追趕　　mouse〔maʊs〕n. 老鼠
fortunately〔ˈfɔrtʃənɪtlɪ〕adv. 幸運地
be able to V. 能夠…　　hole〔hol〕n. 洞
mean〔min〕adj. 卑鄙的;兇惡的
outside〔ˈaʊtˈsaɪd〕prep. 在…外面
suddenly〔ˈsʌdn̩lɪ〕adv. 突然地　　bark〔bɑrk〕v. 吠叫
loudly〔ˈlaʊdlɪ〕adv. 大聲地　　hide〔haɪd〕v. 躲藏
meanwhile〔ˈminˌhwaɪl〕adv. 在此時;同時
inside〔ɪnˈsaɪd〕prep. 在…裡面
practice〔ˈpræktɪs〕v. 練習
language〔ˈlæŋgwɪdʒ〕n. 語言　　fool〔ful〕v. 欺騙
bilingual〔baɪˈlɪŋgwəl〕adj. 能說兩種語言的

口說能力測驗詳解

* 請在 15 秒內完成並唸出下列自我介紹的句子，請開始。

My seat number is （複試座位號碼後 5 碼）, and my test
number is （初試准考證號碼後 5 碼）.

I. 複誦

共五題。題目不印在試卷上，由耳機播出，
每題播出兩次，兩次之間大約有一到二秒的
間隔。聽完兩次後，請馬上複誦一次。

1. Can you finish the work by Friday?
   你能在星期五之前完成工作嗎？

2. Let's get something to drink. 我們買點東西喝吧。

3. Are you going to the library today or tomorrow?
   你是今天要去圖書館還是明天？

4. Hurry up! We're going to be late.
   快點！我們要遲到了。

5. What would you like to do today?
   你今天想要做什麼？

【註】 finish〔'fɪnɪʃ〕v. 完成　　by〔baɪ〕prep. 在…之前
　　　get〔gɛt〕v. 買　　library〔'laɪ,brɛrɪ〕n. 圖書館
　　　hurry up 趕快　　late〔let〕adj. 遲到的

II. 朗讀句子與短文

共有五個句子及一篇短文，請先利用一分
鐘的時間閱讀試卷上的句子與短文，然後
在一分鐘內以正常的速度，清楚正確地朗
讀一遍，請開始閱讀。

One　　: Here is that report you asked for.
　　　　　這是你要的報告。

Two　　: Are you going to buy a new car?
　　　　　你要買新車嗎？

Three　: Robert lives on First Street, close to the school.
　　　　　羅伯特住在第一街，離學校很近。

Four　　: We have to leave now, don't we?
　　　　　我們現在必須離開，不是嗎？

Five　　: When did you receive the package?
　　　　　你何時收到那個包裹？

【註】 report〔rɪ'port〕n. 報告　　***ask for*** 要求
　　　close〔klos〕*adj.* 接近的 < *to* >
　　　receive〔rɪ'siv〕*v.* 收到
　　　package〔'pækɪdʒ〕*n.* 包裹

Six　: Holidays are fun, but shopping for presents can be a lot of trouble. Before you go on a big holiday shopping trip, be sure to put on your most comfortable shoes. Also, shop during the week if you can. This way you will avoid the weekend crowds. Finally, buy the heaviest gifts last so that you don't have to carry them around with you.

假期很有趣，但是購買禮物可能很麻煩。在你進行重要節日購物行程前，一定要穿上最舒服的鞋子。此外，如果可以的話，要在平日購物。這樣你就可以避開週末的人潮。最後，最重的禮物最後才買，如此你就不必帶著它們到處走。

【註】holiday〔'hɑləˌde〕*n.* 假日　　fun〔fʌn〕*adj.* 有趣的
shop for 購買　　present〔'prɛznt〕*n.* 禮物
trouble〔'trʌbl̩〕*n.* 麻煩　　***go on a trip*** 去旅行
be sure to V. 務必⋯　　***put on*** 穿上
comfortable〔'kʌmfə-təbl̩〕*adj.* 舒服的
also〔'ɔlso〕*adv.* 此外　　***during the week*** 在平日
this way 這樣一來　　avoid〔ə'vɔɪd〕*v.* 避開
weekend〔'wik'ɛnd〕*n.* 週末　　crowd〔kraud〕*n.* 人群
finally〔'faɪnl̩ɪ〕*adv.* 最後　　heavy〔'hɛvɪ〕*adj.* 重的
gift〔gɪft〕*n.* 禮物　　***so that*** 以便於；所以
carry〔'kærɪ〕*v.* 攜帶；搬運
around〔ə'raund〕*adv.* 到處

Ⅲ. 回答問題

共七題。題目不印在試卷上，由耳機播出，
每題播出兩次，兩次之間大約有一到二秒的
間隔。聽完兩次後，請馬上回答。每題回答
時間為 15 秒，請在作答時間內儘量地表達。

1. **Q** : Did you come here by yourself or did someone come with you? 你是自己來這裡，還是有人和你一起來？

   A1: I came alone. My parents are busy today. I'll call them when the test is over.
   我自己來的。我的父母今天很忙。當測驗結束後，我會打電話給他們。

   A2: I came with one of my friends. She is taking the test, too. We'll go out for a meal when it's over.
   我和一個朋友一起來的。她也要參加考試。考試結束後，我們會一起出去吃飯。

   【註】 *by oneself* 自己；獨自　　alone〔ə'lon〕*adv.* 獨自
   take a test 參加考試　　meal〔mil〕*n.* 一餐
   go out for a meal 出去吃飯

2. **Q** : What would you like to do on your next holiday?
   你下一個節日想要做什麼？

   A1: I'd really like to go abroad. I've never been before. I think it would be a great experience.
   我很想要出國。我以前從未出過國。我想那會是個很棒的經驗。

A2: I want to take it easy.　I want to completely relax.
Maybe I'll spend my days at the beach.

我想放輕鬆。我想要完全地放鬆。也許我那幾天都會在海
灘上度過。

【註】 abroad〔əˈbrɔd〕*adv.* 到國外　　***go abroad*** 出國
experience〔ɪkˈspɪrɪəns〕*n.* 經驗　　***take it easy*** 放輕鬆
completely〔kəmˈplitlɪ〕*adv.* 完全地
relax〔rɪˈlæks〕*v.* 放鬆　　spend〔spɛnd〕*v.* 度過

3. **Q**：Have you ever seen snow?　你曾經看過雪嗎？

A1: Yes, I saw it in Europe.　I was on a tour of
Switzerland.　Even though it was summer, there was
still some snow in the high mountains.

是的，我在歐洲看過。當時我是去瑞士旅行。即使那時是
夏天，在高山上仍然有一些雪。

A2: No, I've never seen it.　It's pretty rare here because
this is a warm country.　I hope I get the chance to see
it someday.

不，我從未看過雪。雪在這裡很罕見，因為這裡是溫暖的
國家。我希望將來有一天我能有機會看到。

【註】 snow〔sno〕*n.* 雪　　Europe〔ˈjurəp〕*n.* 歐洲
tour〔tur〕*n.* 旅遊
Switzerland〔ˈswɪtsələnd〕*n.* 瑞士
even though 即使　　mountain〔ˈmauntṇ〕*n.* 山
pretty〔ˈprɪtɪ〕*adv.* 相當　　rare〔rɛr〕*adj.* 罕見的
warm〔wɔrm〕*adj.* 溫暖的　　country〔ˈkʌntrɪ〕*n.* 國家
hope〔hop〕*v.* 希望　　chance〔tʃæns〕*n.* 機會
someday〔ˈsʌm͵de〕*adv.* 將來有一天

4. **Q** : Do you like outdoor activities?

你喜歡戶外活動嗎？

A1: Yes, I love being outdoors. I like camping, swimming, and fishing. I often go camping with my family in the summer.

是的，我很喜愛待在戶外。我喜歡露營、游泳，和釣魚。在夏天我常和家人一起去露營。

A2: Actually, I prefer to stay indoors. I don't like sports or getting too hot or too cold. I hate to be uncomfortable.

事實上，我比較喜歡待在室內。我不喜歡運動，或是太熱或太冷。我討厭不舒服。

【註】 outdoor〔'aut,dor〕*adj.* 戶外的
outdoors〔'aut'dorz〕*adv.* 在戶外
camp〔kæmp〕*v.* 露營　　fish〔fɪʃ〕*v.* 釣魚
actually〔'æktʃuəlɪ〕*adv.* 事實上
prefer〔prɪ'fɝ〕*v.* 比較喜歡　　stay〔ste〕*v.* 停留
indoors〔'ɪn'dorz〕*adv.* 在室內　　hate〔het〕*v.* 討厭
uncomfortable〔ʌn'kʌmfɚtəbl̩〕*adj.* 不舒服的

5. **Q** : Which do you like better, listening to live music or a recording?

你比較喜歡哪一個，聽現場的音樂或是錄製的唱片？

A1: I like listening to live music. It sounds so much better than a recording. I also like watching the musicians play.

我喜歡聽現場的音樂。聽起來比錄的唱片好很多。我也喜歡看音樂家演奏。

A2: I'd rather listen to a recording. It sounds better, and I can listen whenever I want. I always have my MP3 player with me.

我寧願聽錄製的唱片。聽起來比較好,而且我可以想聽的時候就聽。我總是隨身帶著 MP3 播放器。

【註】*like better* 比較喜歡　　live〔laɪv〕*adj.* 現場的
recording〔rɪ'kɔrdɪŋ〕*n.* 唱片;錄製品
sound〔saʊnd〕*v.* 聽起來
musician〔mju'zɪʃən〕*n.* 音樂家　　play〔ple〕*v.* 演奏
would rather 寧願　　player〔'pleɚ〕*n.* 播放器

6. **Q**：Please describe what you are wearing today.
請描述你今天的穿著。

A1：I have my favorite T-shirt on. I always wear it for luck when I take a test. I'm also wearing jeans and sneakers.

我穿了我最喜愛的 T 恤。每當我參加考試,我總是穿著它,希望能很幸運。我也穿了牛仔褲和運動鞋。

A2：I'm wearing a blue skirt and a white blouse. I also have a jacket, but I took it off when I came inside. My shoes are comfortable low-heeled shoes.

我穿著一條藍色的裙子,和一件白色的上衣。我也穿了夾克,但是我進來裡面時脫掉了。我的鞋子是舒適的低跟鞋。

【註】describe〔dɪ'skraɪb〕*v.* 描述
favorite〔'fevərɪt〕*adj.* 最喜愛的
T-shirt〔'ti,ʃɜt〕*n.* T 恤　　on〔ɑn〕*adj.* 穿著的
luck〔lʌk〕*n.* 幸運　　jeans〔dʒinz〕*n. pl.* 牛仔褲
sneakers〔'snikəz〕*n. pl.* 運動鞋
blouse〔blaʊs〕*n.* 女用上衣　　jacket〔'dʒækɪt〕*n.* 夾克

take off 脫掉　　inside〔ˈɪnˈsaɪd〕*adv.* 到裡面
low-heeled〔ˌloˈhild〕*adj.* 低跟的

7. **Q** : Your car broke down while you were driving and you call a mechanic. What could you say to him or her?
當你正在開車的時候，你的車子拋錨了，於是你打電話給技工。你能對他或她說什麼？

A1: I'd say, "I'm having some car trouble." Then I'd tell him where I was. I'd ask him to come as soon as possible.
我會說：「我的車子故障了。」然後我會告訴他我在哪裡。我會請他儘快過來。

A2: I could say, "Can you tow my car? It suddenly stopped running, and I don't know why. Please come as soon as you can."
我可以說：「你能幫我拖車嗎？它突然停止運作，我不知道為什麼。請你儘快過來。」

【註】*break down* 拋錨
mechanic〔məˈkænɪk〕*n.* 技工；機械工人
trouble〔ˈtrʌbl̩〕*n.* 麻煩；故障
as soon as possible 儘快（ = *as soon as one can*）
tow〔to〕*v.* 拖　　run〔rʌn〕*v.* 運作

＊請將下列自我介紹的句子再唸一遍，請開始。

My seat number is (複試座位號碼後 5 碼), and my test number is (初試准考證號碼後 5 碼).

初級英語檢定複試測驗 ⑧ 詳解

寫作能力測驗詳解

第一部份：單句寫作

第 1～5 題：句子改寫

1. Sally likes to listen to music.
   Sally enjoys ＿＿＿＿＿＿＿＿＿＿＿＿＿＿＿＿＿＿＿.

   > 重點結構：enjoy 的用法
   >
   > 解　答：Sally enjoys listening to music.
   >
   > 句型分析：主詞＋enjoy＋V-ing＋介系詞＋受詞
   >
   > 説　明：enjoy（享受；喜歡）後面須接名詞或動名詞。
   > 　　　　本句的句意爲：「莎莉喜歡聽音樂。」

2. Matt and Joe often skate in the park.
   Billy often ＿＿＿＿＿＿＿＿＿＿＿＿＿＿＿＿ in the park.

   > 重點結構：複數主詞改爲單數主詞
   >
   > 解　答：Billy often skates in the park.
   >
   > 句型分析：主詞＋頻率副詞＋動詞＋地方副詞
   >
   > 説　明：原句的主詞爲 Matt and Joe，故動詞 skate 不加
   > 　　　　s。複數主詞改爲單數主詞 Billy，則動詞 skate 須
   > 　　　　改爲 skates。本句的句意爲：「比利常常在公園溜
   > 　　　　冰。」
   >
   > ＊ skate〔sket〕v. 溜冰

3. It's going to rain.

Do you think _____?

重點結構：名詞子句的用法

解　答：<u>Do you think (that) it's going to rain?</u>

句型分析：Do you think + (that) + 主詞 + be going to + 原形
　　　　　動詞？

說　明：本句的句意為：「你覺得會下雨嗎？」可用從屬連
　　　　　接詞 that 引導名詞子句，做 think 的受詞，即「連
　　　　　接詞＋主詞＋動詞」，而當 that 子句做受詞時，
　　　　　that 常省略。

4. I didn't make a salad because there was no lettuce.

I didn't make a salad because _____ tomatoes.

重點結構：單數名詞改為複數名詞

解　答：<u>I didn't make a salad because there were no</u>
　　　　　<u>tomatoes.</u>

句型分析：I didn't make a salad because + there + be 動詞
　　　　　＋ not ＋名詞

說　明：原句的 lettuce 為單數名詞，故用過去式單數 be 動
　　　　　詞 was，而名詞改成 tomatoes 為複數名詞，則 be
　　　　　動詞須用過去式複數 were。本句的句意為：「因為
　　　　　沒有蕃茄，所以我沒做沙拉。」

＊ salad〔'sæləd〕n. 沙拉　　lettuce〔'lɛtɪs〕n. 萵苣
　tomato〔tə'meto〕n. 蕃茄

5. We have to complete the assignment today.

We _____ complete the assignment last week.

重點結構：現在式改爲過去式

解　答：<u>We had to complete the assignment last week.</u>

句型分析：主詞＋had to＋原形動詞＋受詞＋時間副詞

説　明：由時間副詞 last week 可知，本句爲過去式，故須將 have to 改成 had to。本句的句意爲：「我們上星期必須完成作業。」

＊ complete〔kəm'plit〕v. 完成

assignment〔ə'saɪnmənt〕n. 作業；功課

第 6～10 題：句子合併

6. The Clarks live in a big house.

The house is old.

The Clarks ＿＿＿＿＿＿＿＿＿＿＿＿＿＿＿＿＿＿＿＿＿＿.

重點結構：形容詞的排序

解　答：<u>The Clarks live in a big old house.</u>

句型分析：主詞＋動詞＋介系詞＋受詞

説　明：本句的句意爲：「克拉克一家人住在一間很大的舊房子裡。」big（大的）以及 old（舊的）都是用來形容 house（房子）的形容詞，當有數個形容詞用來修飾相同名詞時，排列順序大致如下：大小/長短/形狀 → 新舊 → 顏色 → 國籍 → 材料。

7. Jason wants to be a doctor.

Jason wants to work in a hospital.

Jason ＿＿＿＿＿＿＿＿＿＿＿＿ and ＿＿＿＿＿＿＿＿＿＿＿＿.

重點結構：and 的用法

解　答：<u>Jason wants to be a doctor and work in a</u>
　　　　<u>hospital.</u>

句型分析：主詞＋ want to ＋原形動詞 A ＋ and ＋原形動詞 B ＋
　　　　　地方副詞

說　明：提示中有兩個動詞片語：be a doctor 和 work in a
　　　　　hospital，用對等連接詞 and 來連接。本句的句意
　　　　　爲：「傑森想當醫生並且在醫院工作。」

* hospital〔ˈhɑspɪtl̩〕n. 醫院

8. We ran out of the theater.

　　The fire alarm rang.

　　As soon as ＿＿＿＿＿＿＿＿＿＿＿＿＿＿＿＿ theater.

重點結構：as soon as 的用法

解　答：<u>As soon as the fire alarm rang, we ran out of</u>
　　　　<u>the theater.</u>

句型分析：As soon as ＋主詞＋動詞＋，＋主詞＋動詞＋副詞
　　　　　片語

說　明：本句的句意爲：「當火災警鈴一響，我們就從戲院
　　　　　裡跑出來。」as soon as 表示「一…就～」，引導
　　　　　副詞子句，修飾動詞 ran。

* ***as soon as*** 一…就～　　alarm〔əˈlɑrm〕n. 警鈴
　fire alarm 火災警鈴　　ring〔rɪŋ〕v.（鈴）響
　run out of 跑出　　　　theater〔ˈθiətɚ〕n. 戲院；電影院

9. I went to the library.

　　Amy told me where it was.

　　Amy told ＿＿＿＿＿＿＿＿＿＿＿＿＿＿＿＿＿.

重點結構：間接問句的用法

解　答：<u>Amy told me where the library was.</u>

句型分析：主詞＋動詞＋間接受詞＋直接受詞（疑問詞＋主詞＋動詞）

說　明：Amy told me 後面的間接問句 where it was 是直接受詞，依句意，it 是指 the library，故寫成：where the library is。本句的句意為：「艾咪告訴我圖書館在哪裡。」

* library〔'laɪ͵brɛrɪ〕n. 圖書館

10. I go to the park.
   I go every time I have free time.
   _____ whenever _____.

重點結構：whenever 的用法

解　答：<u>I go to the park whenever I have free time.</u>

句型分析：主詞＋動詞＋介系詞＋受詞＋whenever＋主詞＋動詞＋受詞

說　明：本句的句意為：「每當我有空閒時間，我就會去公園。」連接詞 whenever 表示「每當⋯的時候」，引導表時間的副詞子句，修飾動詞 go。

* *every time* 每次　　*free time* 空閒時間

第 11～15 題：重組

11. The people _____.
   from Spain / live / who / door / are / next

重點結構：關係代名詞 who 的用法

解　答：<u>The people who live next door are from Spain.</u>

句型分析：主詞（先行詞）＋關代（who）＋動詞＋地方副詞
　　　　　＋be 動詞＋介系詞＋受詞

説　明：先行詞為人，故關係代名詞用 who，引導形容詞子
　　　　句，修飾 The people。本句的句意為：「住在我們
　　　　隔壁的人是從西班牙來的。」

* **next door** （在）隔壁　　Spain〔spen〕*n.* 西班牙

12. The ＿＿＿＿＿＿＿＿＿＿＿＿＿＿＿＿＿＿＿＿＿＿＿.
　　too expensive / , so / by train / air ticket / we / went / was

重點結構：so 的用法

解　答：<u>The air ticket was too expensive, so we went by
　　　　train.</u>

句型分析：主詞＋be 動詞＋副詞＋形容詞＋, ＋so＋主詞＋
　　　　　動詞＋by＋交通工具

説　明：連接詞 because 和 so 的比較：

　　　　$\begin{cases} 結果＋because＋原因 \\ 原因＋so＋結果 \end{cases}$

　　　　原因是「機票太貴了」，結果是「我們搭火車去」，
　　　　so 前面放原因，後面放結果。

* **air ticket** 機票　　expensive〔ɪk'spɛnsɪv〕*adj.* 昂貴的

13. Were ＿＿＿＿＿＿＿＿＿＿＿＿＿＿＿＿＿＿＿＿?
　　book / you / to / the / find / able

重點結構：be able to 的用法

解　答：Were you able to find the book?

句型分析：be 動詞＋主詞＋able to＋原形動詞＋受詞？

說　明：be able to 表示「能夠～」，後面接原形動詞。
因為是疑問句，故主詞和動詞須倒裝，本句的句意為：「你能夠找到那本書嗎？」

14. Mr. and Mrs. _____.
　　to / a / Lee / car / buy / new / want

重點結構：want 的用法

解　答：Mr. and Mrs. Lee want to buy a new car.

句型分析：主詞＋動詞＋不定詞＋受詞

說　明：want 表示「想要」，後須接不定詞 to V.。本句的句意為：「李先生和李太太想要買一台新車。」

15. We _____.
　　go to / restaurants / often / nice / don't

重點結構：頻率副詞的用法

解　答：We don't often go to nice restaurants.

句型分析：主詞＋否定助動詞＋頻率副詞＋一般動詞＋介系詞
＋形容詞＋名詞

說　明：often 為頻率副詞，須放在主要動詞前或 be 動詞
後，本句的句意為：「我們不常去很好的餐廳。」

* nice〔naɪs〕adj. 好的　　restaurant〔'rɛstərənt〕n. 餐廳

第二部份：段落寫作

題目： Little Rabbit 喜歡吃甜食。請根據以下的圖片寫一篇約 50 字
的短文。**注意：未依提示作答者，將予扣分。**

Little Rabbit had a sweet tooth. He loved to eat candy,
cake, and cookies. ***But one day*** he had a terrible toothache.
He went to see the dentist, and the dentist found several
holes in his teeth. He told Little Rabbit that he had to brush
his teeth more often. The dentist also said that he could not
eat sweets anymore. Poor Little Rabbit was very sad.

小兔很喜歡吃甜食。他很愛吃糖果、蛋糕，和餅乾。但是有一
天，他牙齒很痛。他去看牙醫，而牙醫發現他的牙齒有好幾個洞。
他告訴小兔，他必須更常刷牙。牙醫也說他不能再吃甜食了。可憐
的小兔非常傷心。

rabbit〔ˋræbɪt〕n. 兔子　　tooth〔tuθ〕n. 牙齒
have a sweet tooth 喜歡吃甜食　　candy〔ˋkændɪ〕n. 糖果
cookie〔ˋkʊkɪ〕n. 餅乾　　terrible〔ˋtɛrəbḷ〕adj. 嚴重的
toothache〔ˋtuθ͵ek〕n. 牙痛　　dentist〔ˋdɛntɪst〕n. 牙醫
hole〔hol〕n. 洞　　brush〔brʌʃ〕v. 刷
not…anymore 不再；再也不　　sweets〔swits〕n. pl. 甜食
sad〔sæd〕adj. 悲傷的

口說能力測驗詳解

* 請在 15 秒內完成並唸出下列自我介紹的句子，請開始。

My seat number is (複試座位號碼後 5 碼) , and my test number is (初試准考證號碼後 5 碼) .

I. 複誦

共五題。題目不印在試卷上，由耳機播出，
每題播出兩次，兩次之間大約有一到二秒的
間隔。聽完兩次後，請馬上複誦一次。

1. Are you taking French or Spanish this year?
   你今年要修法文還是西班牙文？

2. Wait a second. I'll be right there.　等一下。我馬上到。

3. You can't use your phone here.
   你不能在這裡使用你的電話。

4. What time does the concert start?　演唱會什麼時候開始？

5. Is this the book you were looking for?
   這是你在找的那本書嗎？

【註】 take〔tek〕v. 修（課）　　French〔frɛntʃ〕n. 法文
　　　Spanish〔spænɪʃ〕n. 西班牙文
　　　second〔'sɛkənd〕n. 秒；片刻；一會兒
　　　wait a second 等一下　　right〔raɪt〕adv. 立刻；馬上
　　　concert〔'kɑnsɝt〕n. 音樂會；演唱會　　***look for*** 尋找

II. 朗讀句子與短文

共有五個句子及一篇短文，請先利用一分
鐘的時間閱讀試卷上的句子與短文，然後
在一分鐘內以正常的速度，清楚正確地朗
讀一遍，請開始閱讀。

One : Did you remember to bring your ID card?

你有記得帶你的身份證嗎？

Two : Which of these DVDs would you like to watch first?

這些 DVD 你想要先看哪一個？

Three : I'm afraid you'll have to work late tonight.

恐怕你今晚必須要工作到很晚。

Four : This book, which I read last month, is very good.

這本書我上個月看過，非常好。

Five : Betty can sing very well, can't she?

貝蒂很會唱歌，不是嗎？

【註】 remember〔 rɪˋmɛmbɚ 〕v. 記得
   ID card 身分證   first〔 fɝst 〕adv. 先
   I'm afraid 恐怕   late〔 let 〕adv. 晚；到很晚
   month〔 mʌnθ 〕n. 月

Six : A bad sunburn can seriously damage your skin.
You can prevent sunburn by avoiding the sun
between 10 a.m. and 3 p.m. That is when the sun is
strongest. In addition, use sunscreen whenever you
go outdoors, and reapply every two or three hours.
Also, wear a hat to protect both your scalp and your
face. Finally, wear sunglasses to protect your eyes.

過度的曬傷可能會嚴重損害你的皮膚。你可以藉由避開
早上十點到下午三點之間的太陽，來預防曬傷。那時是
太陽最強烈的時刻。此外，每當外出時，都要擦防曬乳，
並且每兩或三小時要再補擦。而且，戴帽子能保護你的
頭皮和臉。最後，要戴太陽眼鏡保護你的眼睛。

【註】 bad〔bæd〕*adj.* 嚴重的　　sunburn〔'sʌn,bɜn〕*n.* 曬傷
seriously〔'sɪrɪəslɪ〕*adj.* 嚴重的
damage〔'dæmɪdʒ〕*v.* 損害　　skin〔skɪn〕*n.* 皮膚
prevent〔prɪ'vɛnt〕*v.* 預防　　avoid〔ə'vɔɪd〕*v.* 避開
the sun 太陽　　***in addition*** 另外
sunscreen〔'sʌn,skrin〕*n.* 防曬油；放曬霜
outdoors〔'aʊt'dorz〕*adv.* 在戶外；向戶外
reapply〔,riə'plaɪ〕*v.* 再塗上　　also〔'ɔlso〕*adv.* 此外
protect〔prə'tɛkt〕*v.* 保護　　scalp〔skælp〕*n.* 頭皮
sunglasses〔'sʌn,glæsɪz〕*n. pl.* 太陽眼鏡

Ⅲ. 回答問題

共七題。題目不印在試卷上，由耳機播出，
每題播出兩次，兩次之間大約有一到二秒的
間隔。聽完兩次後，請馬上回答。每題回答
時間為 15 秒，請在作答時間內儘量地表達。

1. **Q**：Did you run into any traffic on the way here today?
　　你今天來這裡時有遇到任何交通狀況嗎？

　A1：No, I didn't. I left after rush hour. The roads were
　　　pretty clear.
　　　不，我沒有。我在尖峰時間之後才離開。道路很暢通。

　A2：Yes, I did. I ran into a terrible traffic jam. I was
　　　really worried that I was going to be late.
　　　是的，我有。我遇到嚴重的交通阻塞。我很擔心我可能會
　　　遲到。

　【註】***run into*** 偶然遇到　　traffic〔ˈtræfɪk〕*n.* 交通
　　　on the way here 來這裡的途中
　　　rush hour 尖峰時間　　pretty〔ˈprɪtɪ〕*adv.* 相當
　　　clear〔klɪr〕*adv.* 暢通的；無障礙的
　　　traffic jam 交通阻塞　　worried〔ˈwɜɪd〕*adj.* 擔心的

2. **Q**：What do you look like? Please describe yourself.
　　你看起來如何？請描述你自己。

　A1：I'm average height and build. I have short dark hair.
　　　My eyes are big and my nose is small.

我的身高和體格很一般。我有黑色的短髮。我的眼睛很大，
鼻子很小。

A2: I'm a little on the short side. I have long straight hair.
My friends say I have a nice smile.

我有一點矮。我留長直髮。我的朋友都說我笑起來很好看。

【註】describe〔dɪ'skraɪb〕v. 描述
average〔'ævərɪdʒ〕adj. 平均的；一般的
height〔haɪt〕n. 身高　　build〔bɪld〕n. 體格
dark〔dɑrk〕adj. (頭髮) 帶黑色的
be on the short side 太矮
straight〔stret〕adj. 直的

3. **Q** : How is the weather today?

今天的天氣如何？

A1: Today is a little cooler than usual. It's overcast and
pretty humid. I think it might rain later.

今天比平常涼了一點。天氣多雲，而且相當潮濕。我想待
會可能會下雨。

A2: Today is clear and sunny. The temperature is around
25 degrees. It's really a nice day!

今天天氣晴朗而且陽光充足。溫度大約 25 度。今天真是很
棒的一天！

【註】weather〔'wɛðə〕n. 天氣　　cool〔kul〕adj. 涼爽的
than usual 比平常
overcast〔'ovə,kæst〕adj. 多雲的
humid〔'hjumɪd〕adj. 潮濕的
later〔'letə〕adv. 待會　　clear〔klɪr〕adj. 晴朗的

sunny〔'sʌnɪ〕*adj.* 晴朗的；陽光充足的
temperature〔'tɛmpərətʃɚ〕*n.* 溫度
around〔ə'raʊnd〕*adv.* 大約　　degree〔dɪ'gri〕*n.* 度

4. **Q** : What do you like to do for fun?
 你喜歡做什麼休閒活動？

A1: I like to surf the Net and play computer games. I can stay online for hours. I have to limit myself so that I don't waste too much time.
 我喜歡上網和玩電腦遊戲。我可以在線上待好幾個小時。
 我必須限制自己，這樣才不會浪費太多時間。

A2: I like to do something active like go for a run. Most people don't think that's fun, but I do. It makes me feel healthy and strong.
 我喜歡做些動態的事，像是去跑步。大部分的人不認為那很有趣，但我覺得有趣。跑步讓我覺得健康又強壯。

【註】*for fun* 為了好玩　　surf〔sɝf〕*v.* 瀏覽（網路）
 the Net 網際網路（= *the Internet*）
 surf the Net 上網　　stay〔ste〕*v.* 停留
 online〔'ɑn,laɪn〕*adv.* 在線上　　limit〔'lɪmɪt〕*v.* 限制
 so that 以便於　　waste〔west〕*v.* 浪費
 active〔'æktɪv〕*adj.* 活躍的；主動的　　run〔rʌn〕*n.* 跑
 go for a run 去跑步　　fun〔fʌn〕*adj.* 有趣的
 healthy〔'hɛlθɪ〕*adj.* 健康的

5. **Q** : How often do you go out to eat? Who do you usually go with?
 你多久出去吃一次飯？你通常和誰一起去？

A1: I eat out every day. On weekdays, I have dinner with my classmates. On weekends, I eat out with my family.

我每天都去外面吃。平日我會和同學一起吃晚餐。週末時，我會和家人去外面吃。

A2: I rarely eat out. My mother likes to cook, so we usually eat at home. But sometimes I have lunch out with a friend on Saturday.

我很少去外面吃。我媽媽喜歡煮飯，所以我們通常在家吃。但在星期六，有時我會和朋友出去吃午餐。

【註】out〔aut〕*adv.* 在外面　　***eat out*** 去外面吃
　　　weekday〔'wik,de〕*n.* 平日　　have〔hæv〕*v.* 吃
　　　weekend〔'wik'ɛnd〕*n.* 週末
　　　rarely〔'rɛrlı〕*adv.* 很少　　cook〔kʊk〕*v.* 做菜

6. **Q**：Have you ever been swimming in the ocean?

你曾經在海裡游過泳嗎？

A1：Yes, many times. I often go to the beach in the summer. I enjoy playing in the water.

是的，很多次。我夏天常去海邊。我很喜歡在水裡玩。

A2：No, I never have. But I do know how to swim. I swim in my community pool three times a week.

不，我從沒去過。但是我真的知道如何游泳。我一星期會在我們社區游泳池游三次。

【註】ocean〔'oʃən〕*n.* 海洋　　time〔taım〕*n.* 次
　　　beach〔bitʃ〕*n.* 海邊
　　　do know 真的知道【do 可用於強調肯定句】

community〔kə'mjunətɪ〕 n. 社區
pool〔pul〕 n. 游泳池

7. **Q** : Your neighbor is playing music very loudly. What can you say to him?

你的鄰居音樂播放得很大聲，你可以和他說什麼？

A1: I might be angry, but I'd try to stay calm. I'd say, "Could you turn it down, please? It's quite loud, and I'm trying to sleep."

我可能會生氣，但是我會試著保持冷靜。我會說：「可以請你關小聲一點嗎？音樂相當大聲，而我正想要睡覺。」

A2: I'd say, "Excuse me, but your music is disturbing me. I'm trying to study, but your music is too loud. Please be considerate and turn it down."

我會說：「不好意思，你的音樂打擾到我了。我想要讀書，但是你的音樂太大聲了。請你體諒，把它關小聲一點。」

【註】 neighbor〔'nebɚ〕 n. 鄰居　　play〔ple〕 v. 播放
loudly〔'laʊdlɪ〕 adv. 大聲地　　stay〔ste〕 v. 保持
calm〔kɑm〕 adj. 冷靜的　　***turn down*** 關小聲
loud〔laʊd〕 adj. 大聲的　　***try to V.*** 試圖…；想要…
disturb〔dɪ'stɝb〕 v. 打擾
considerate〔kən'sɪdərɪt〕 adj. 體貼的

*請將下列自我介紹的句子再唸一遍，請開始。

My seat number is （複試座位號碼後 5 碼），and my test
number is （初試准考證號碼後 5 碼）.

初級英語檢定複試測驗⑨詳解

寫作能力測驗詳解

第一部份：單句寫作

第 1∼5 題：句子改寫

1. Tammy and Larry sometimes drink tea in the afternoon.
   Tammy and Larry ＿＿＿＿＿＿＿＿＿＿＿＿＿＿ tea yesterday.

   重點結構：現在式改爲過去式

   解　答：Tammy and Larry drank tea yesterday.

   句型分析：主詞 A ＋ and ＋ 主詞 B ＋ 動詞 ＋ 受詞 ＋ 時間副詞

   説　明：由 yesterday 可知爲過去式，故動詞須改爲 drank。
   本句的句意爲：「湯米和賴瑞昨天喝茶。」

2. On the sofa, there are two pillows.
   On the sofa, ＿＿＿＿＿＿＿＿＿＿＿＿＿＿＿ pillow.

   重點結構：複數名詞改爲單數名詞

   解　答：On the sofa, there is a/one pillow.

   句型分析：地方副詞 ＋ , ＋ there is/are ＋ 名詞

   説　明：there is/are 表示「有」，本句的句意爲：「在沙發
   上有一顆枕頭。」由複數名詞 two pillows 改爲單
   數名詞 a/one pillow，故 be 動詞 are 也須改爲 is。

   ＊ sofa〔'sofə〕n. 沙發　　　pillow〔'pɪlo〕n. 枕頭

3. We must go home by ten o'clock now.

We _____ go home by ten o'clock when we were children.

    重點結構：現在式改為過去式

      解   答：<u>We had to go home by ten o'clock when we</u>
             <u>were children.</u>

    句型分析：主詞＋had to＋原形動詞＋地方副詞＋時間副詞＋
             when＋主詞＋be動詞＋補語

      說   明：由 when we were children 可知為過去式，故助動
             詞 must 須改為 had to（必須）。本句的句意為：
             「在我們小時候，我們必須十點之前回家。」

    * by〔baɪ〕*prep.* 在⋯之前

4. Are you going to the cram school today?

_____ yesterday?

    重點結構：現在進行式改為過去式

      解   答：<u>Did you go to the cram school yesterday?</u>

    句型分析：Did＋主詞＋原形動詞＋介系詞＋受詞＋時間副詞？

      說   明：現在進行式改為過去式，故 Are you going to 須改
             為 Did you go to。本句的句意為：「你昨天有去補
             習班嗎？」

    * *cram school* 補習班

5. Johnny, put the pencil on the table.

Johnny _____ it _____.

    重點結構：命令句改為直述句

解　答：<u>Johnny put it on the table.</u>

句型分析：主詞＋動詞＋受詞＋地方副詞

説　明：命令句改為直述句，依句意為過去式，而 put 三態
　　　　同形，故動詞用 put，用代名詞 it 代替 the pencil。
　　　　本句的句意為：「強尼把它放在桌上。」

第 6～10 題：句子合併

6. Jim wants to buy a large car.
   There are six people in his family.
   Because ＿＿＿＿＿＿＿＿＿＿＿＿＿＿＿＿＿＿＿＿＿．

重點結構：Because 的用法

解　答：<u>Because there are six people in his family, Jim
　　　　wants to buy a large car.</u>

句型分析：Because＋there＋be 動詞＋名詞＋地方副詞＋,＋
　　　　主詞＋動詞＋不定詞＋受詞

説　明：本句的句意為：「因為家裡有六個人，所以吉姆想
　　　　要買一輛大車。」Because 引導副詞子句，表「原
　　　　因」，修飾主要動詞 wants。

7. I want to send a fax.
   I don't know how to do it.
   I don't know ＿＿＿＿＿＿＿＿＿＿＿＿＿＿＿＿＿＿＿．

重點結構：how 引導名詞片語

解　答：<u>I don't know how to send a fax.</u>

句型分析：主詞＋否定助動詞＋原形動詞＋how＋不定詞＋受詞

說　明：本句的句意為：「我不知道如何傳真。」I don't
　　　　know 後面須接受詞，故用名詞片語 how to send
　　　　a fax。

* fax〔fæks〕*n.* 傳真

8. There are lots of trees in the park.
   Some of the trees are very old.
   There ＿＿＿＿＿＿＿, some of which ＿＿＿＿＿＿＿＿.

　　重點結構：形容詞子句的用法

　　　解　答：<u>There are lots of trees in the park, some of
　　　　　　　which are very old.</u>

　　句型分析：There + be 動詞 + 名詞 + 地方副詞 + , + some of
　　　　　　　+ 關代 + 動詞 + 副詞 + 形容詞

　　　說　明：There + be 動詞，表示「有」，關代所有格 some
　　　　　　　of which，引導形容詞子句，修飾先行詞 trees。
　　　　　　　本句的句意為：「公園裡有很多樹，其中有一些是
　　　　　　　非常老的。」

　　* *lots of* 很多的

9. Here is the magazine you wanted.
   The magazine is new.
   Here ＿＿＿＿＿＿＿＿＿＿＿＿＿.

　　重點結構：形容詞修飾名詞

　　　解　答：<u>Here is the new magazine you wanted.</u>

　　句型分析：地方副詞 + be 動詞 + 定冠詞 + 形容詞 + 名詞 +
　　　　　　　（關代）+ 主詞 + 動詞

說　明：本句的句意爲：「這是你想要的那本新雜誌。」
形容詞 new 置於名詞 magazine 前，修飾名詞。
you wanted 源自 that/which you wanted，又
關代做受詞時可省略，故可寫成 you wanted。

* magazine 〔ˌmægəˈzin 〕 *n.* 雜誌

10. This is the new movie.
Everyone is talking about it.

_____ that _____.

重點結構：關係代名詞 that 的用法

解　答：This is the new movie that everyone is talking about.

句型分析：指示代名詞＋be 動詞＋定冠詞＋形容詞＋名詞＋形容詞子句

說　明：that 引導形容詞子句，修飾先行詞 movie。
本句的句意爲：「這是每個人都在談論的那部新電影。」

* **talk about** 談論

第 11～15 題：重組

11. The _____.

my uncle / jacket / in the / is / blue / man

重點結構：in 的用法

解　答：The man in the blue jacket is my uncle.

句型分析：主詞＋介系詞片語＋be 動詞＋主詞補語

　　　　說　明：in 表「穿著…（衣服）」。本句的句意爲：「那個

　　　　　　　　穿著藍色夾克的男人是我的叔叔。」

　　* jacket〔ˋdʒækɪt〕 n. 夾克

12. Amanda _____.

assignments / late / her / rarely / hands in

　　重點結構：頻率副詞的用法

　　　解　答：Amanda rarely hands in her assignments late.

　　句型分析：主詞＋頻率副詞＋動詞＋受詞＋副詞

　　　說　明：rarely（很少）是頻率副詞，須放在一般動詞前，

　　　　　　　　be 動詞之後。本句的句意爲：「阿曼達很少遲交

　　　　　　　　作業。」

　　* rarely〔ˋrɛrlɪ〕 adv. 很少　　**hand in**　繳交

　　　assignment〔 əˋsaɪnmənt〕 n. 作業　　late〔 let 〕 adv. 遲；晚

13. I _____.

going to / remember / year / the zoo / last

　　重點結構：remember 的用法

　　　解　答：I remember going to the zoo last year.

　　句型分析：主詞＋remember＋V-ing＋介系詞＋受詞＋

　　　　　　　　時間副詞

　　　說　明：本句的句意爲：「我記得去年去了動物園。」

　　　　　　　　remember（記得）的寫法有兩種：

　　　　　　　　⎧ remember＋to V. 記得去做…【動作未完成】
　　　　　　　　⎩ remember＋V-ing 記得做過…【動作已完成】

　　　　　　　　本句爲第二種寫法。

14. Wendy's parents _____.

    lonely / not / she / are / feels / at home / , so

    重點結構：so 的用法

    解　　答：<u>Wendy's parents are not at home, so she feels lonely.</u>

    句型分析：主詞＋be 動詞＋not＋地方副詞＋, ＋so＋主詞＋連綴動詞＋形容詞

    說　　明：用表「結果」的連接詞 so（所以）來連接兩句話。本句的句意為：「溫蒂的父母不在家，所以她覺得寂寞。」

    * lonely〔'lonlɪ〕adj. 寂寞的

15. Are _____.

    Jim's / going / tomorrow / party / to / you

    重點結構：be going to 的用法

    解　　答：<u>Are you going to Jim's party tomorrow?</u>

    句型分析：Are＋主詞＋going to＋受詞＋時間副詞？

    說　　明：be 動詞 Are 置於句首，可知為疑問句，故主詞與動詞須倒裝，又 be going to 是「將要」，故寫成：Are you going to，之後再接 Jim's party，再加時間 tomorrow。本句的句意為：「你明天會去吉姆的派對嗎？」

第二部份：段落寫作

題目： 一位乞丐在街上發現了一袋錢。請根據以下的圖片寫一篇約
50 字的短文。**注意**：未依提示作答者，將予扣分。

    A poor beggar was walking along the street. ***Suddenly***
he found a bag full of money! He didn't know what to do.
Should he keep it or return it to the owner? After struggling
in his mind for a long time, the beggar decided to return the
money. The owner of the bag was very happy, and he gave
the honest beggar a present.

    有個貧窮的乞丐正走在街上。突然間，他發現了一個裝滿錢的
袋子！他不知道該怎麼辦。他應該留下它，還是將它還給物主？在
心中掙扎很久之後，這位乞丐決定將錢歸還。那個袋子的主人很高
興，所以給了那位誠實的乞丐一個禮物。

poor〔pur〕*adj.* 貧窮的   beggar〔'bɛgɚ〕*n.* 乞丐
along〔ə'lɔŋ〕*prep.* 沿著   suddenly〔'sʌdn̩lɪ〕*adv.* 突然地
be full of 充滿了   keep〔kip〕*v.* 保留
return〔rɪ'tɝn〕*v.* 歸還   owner〔'onɚ〕*n.* 擁有者
struggle〔'strʌgl̩〕*v.* 掙扎   mind〔maɪnd〕*n.* 心
decide〔dɪ'saɪd〕*v.* 決定   honest〔'ɑnɪst〕*adj.* 誠實的
present〔'prɛzn̩t〕*n.* 禮物

口說能力測驗詳解

＊請在 15 秒內完成並唸出下列自我介紹的句子，請開始。

My seat number is (複試座位號碼後 5 碼) , and my test
number is (初試准考證號碼後 5 碼) .

I. 複誦

共五題。題目不印在試卷上，由耳機播出，
每題播出兩次，兩次之間大約有一到二秒的
間隔。聽完兩次後，請馬上複誦一次。

1. Sit wherever you like. 你喜歡坐哪裡就坐哪裡。

2. Did you enjoy the movie?
   你喜歡那部電影嗎？

3. Who is playing the piano?
   誰正在彈鋼琴？

4. Be quiet. The baby is sleeping.
   安靜。那個嬰兒正在睡覺。

5. Is Lisa or Donna your best friend?
   你最好的朋友是麗莎還是唐娜？

【註】 wherever〔hwɛr'ɛvɚ〕 conj. 無論何處
enjoy〔ɪn'dʒɔɪ〕 v. 喜歡　　***play the piano*** 彈鋼琴
quiet〔'kwaɪət〕 adj. 安靜的　　baby〔'bebɪ〕 n. 嬰兒

II. 朗讀句子與短文

共有五個句子及一篇短文，請先利用一分
鐘的時間閱讀試卷上的句子與短文，然後
在一分鐘內以正常的速度，清楚正確地朗
讀一遍，請開始閱讀。

One : You haven't been waiting too long, have you?
你沒有等太久，有嗎？

Two : Don't run. The floor is slippery.
不要跑。地板很滑。

Three : Who was that man you were talking to?
和你說話的那個男人是誰？

Four : Bob didn't go to the game, and neither did Joe.
鮑伯沒有去看那場比賽，喬也沒去。

Five : Was the store open when you got there?
你到那裡的時候，那家店有開嗎？

【註】 floor〔flor〕*n.* 地板
slippery〔'slɪpərɪ〕*adj.* 滑的
game〔gem〕*n.* 比賽
neither〔'niðɚ〕*adv.* 也不
open〔'opən〕*adj.* 開著的；營業中的

Six : Keeping a diary is a wonderful way to both practice writing and record your memories. However, it is sometimes hard to find time for it. The best thing to do is schedule a regular time for writing. Then find a quiet place where no one will interrupt you. If you do this, writing in your diary will soon become a regular habit.

寫日記是個很棒的方式，既能練習寫作，又能記錄回憶。然而，有時候要找到時間寫日記很難。最好就是排定一個固定的時間寫。然後找一個沒有人會打斷你，很安靜的地方。如果你這麼做，寫日記很快就會成為你固定的習慣。

【註】 diary〔'daɪərɪ〕*n.* 日記　　***keep a diary*** 寫日記
wonderful〔'wʌndəfəl〕*adj.* 很棒的
way〔we〕*n.* 方式　　practice〔'præktɪs〕*v.* 練習
record〔rɪ'kɔrd〕*v.* 紀錄
memory〔'mɛmərɪ〕*n.* 回憶
sometimes〔'sʌm,taɪmz〕*adv.* 有時候
hard〔hɑrd〕*adj.* 困難的
The best thing to do is V. 最好就是…
schedule〔'skɛdʒul〕*v.* 排定
regular〔'rɛgjələ〕*adj.* 固定的
quiet〔'kwaɪət〕*adj.* 安靜的
interrupt〔,ɪntə'rʌpt〕*v.* 打斷
habit〔'hæbɪt〕*n.* 習慣

Ⅲ. 回答問題

共七題。題目不印在試卷上，由耳機播出，
每題播出兩次，兩次之間大約有一到二秒的
間隔。聽完兩次後，請馬上回答。每題回答
時間為 15 秒，請在作答時間內儘量地表達。

1. **Q**：Is this the first time you have come to this building?
　　這是你第一次來這棟大樓嗎？

　A1：Yes, it is. In fact, I've never been to this part of town
　　　before. But it was easy to find.
　　　是的，是第一次。事實上，我以前從未來過城裡的這個地
　　　區。但是很容易找。

　A2：No, I've been here before. I used to take a class here.
　　　It was a long time ago, though.
　　　不，我以前來過這裡。我以前在這裡上過課。不過那是很
　　　久以前了。

　【註】 time〔taɪm〕*n.* 次　　building〔'bɪldɪŋ〕*n.* 建築物；大樓
　　　　in fact 事實上　　***have never been to*** 從未去過
　　　　part〔part〕*n.* 部份；地區　　town〔taʊn〕*n.* 城鎮
　　　　used to 以前　　***take a class*** 上課
　　　　though〔ðo〕*adv.* 不過【置於句尾】

2. **Q**：Do you like your school or work? Why?
　　你喜歡你的學校或工作嗎？為什麼？

　A1：Yes, I like my school. I have a lot of friends there.
　　　As high schools go, it's not a bad place.

是的，我喜歡我的學校。我在那裡有很多朋友。就高中而言，那是個不錯的地方。

A2: No, not really. The building is very old. Things often break down and it's uncomfortable.

不，不怎麼喜歡。建築物很老舊。東西常常故障，而且很不舒服。

【註】 *high school* 高中　　*as…go* 與普通的…做比較
　　　not really 並沒有；並不是　　*break down* 故障
　　　uncomfortable〔ʌn'kʌmfɚtəbḷ〕*adj.* 不舒服的

3. **Q** : How do you deal with hot weather?

你如何應付炎熱的天氣？

A1: I try to stay cool. I try not to go out during the hottest part of the day. I also drink a lot of water.

我會努力保持涼爽。在一天最炎熱的期間，我會試著不要出去。我也會喝很多水。

A2: I avoid the heat as much as possible. I go to a lot of movies and shopping malls. I also go swimming whenever I can.

我會儘量避開炎熱。我會去看很多電影，並且逛很多購物中心。如果可以的話，我也會去游泳。

【註】 *deal with* 應付；處理　　weather〔'wɛðɚ〕*n.* 天氣
　　　stay〔ste〕*v.* 保持　　cool〔kul〕*adj.* 涼爽的
　　　part〔pɑrt〕*n.* 部份　　avoid〔ə'vɔɪd〕*v.* 避開
　　　heat〔hit〕*n.* 熱　　*as…as possible* 儘可能…
　　　go to a movie 去看電影　　*shopping mall* 購物中心
　　　whenever〔hwɛn'ɛvɚ〕*conj.* 每當…的時候

4. **Q** : Do you enjoy playing sports?

你喜歡運動嗎?

A1: Yes, I love sports. I especially like soccer. I've played it since I was a kid, and now I'm on my school team.

是的,我喜歡運動。我尤其喜歡足球。我從小就踢足球,而且現在我是校隊的成員。

A2: No, I don't like to play sports. I'm not very athletic. I like to watch some sports, though.

不,我不喜歡運動。我不是很擅長運動。不過,我喜歡看一些運動比賽。

【註】 sport〔sport〕*n.* 運動;體育競技
especially〔ə'spɛʃəlɪ〕*adv.* 尤其;特別是
soccer〔'sɑkɚ〕*n.* 足球   team〔tim〕*n.* 隊
athletic〔æθ'lɛtɪk〕*adj.* 擅長運動的

5. **Q** : What would you like to do more, travel in your country or travel abroad?

你比較喜歡做什麼,在你的國家旅行或是出國旅遊?

A1: I'd rather travel in my own country. It's a lot cheaper and less tiring. Besides, there are a lot of wonderful places that I haven't seen yet.

我寧願在我自己的國家旅行。比較便宜,而且比較不累。此外,有很多很棒的地方我還沒看過。

A2: Oh, I'd love to go abroad. I think it would be very exciting. I hope I have the opportunity someday.

喔，我很喜歡出國。我認爲那會很刺激。我希望將來有一天我能有這樣的機會。

【註】 abroad〔ə'brɔd〕adv. 到國外　　**would rather** 寧願
tiring〔'taɪrɪŋ〕adj. 累人的
besides〔bɪ'saɪdz〕adv. 此外
wonderful〔'wʌndəfəl〕adj. 很棒的
not…yet 尚未；還沒　　**go abroad** 出國
exciting〔ɪk'saɪtɪŋ〕adj. 令人興奮的；刺激的
opportunity〔͵ɑpə'tjunətɪ〕n. 機會
someday〔'sʌm͵de〕adv. 將來有一天

6. **Q** : Have you ever been in a traffic accident?
你曾經發生過車禍嗎？

A1 : Yes, I once hit a car with my motorbike. Luckily, it wasn't serious. The driver of the car was angry, but we settled it in the end.
是的，我曾經騎摩托車撞到一輛汽車。幸好並不嚴重。汽車駕駛人很生氣，但我們最後和解了。

A2: No, fortunately I haven't. I'm a very careful driver. I hope I never have to experience that.
不，幸好我沒發生過。我開車很小心。我希望我絕對不需要經歷那件事。

【註】 traffic〔'træfɪk〕n. 交通
accident〔'æksədənt〕n. 意外　　once〔wʌns〕adv. 曾經
hit〔hɪt〕v. 撞上　　motorbike〔'motə͵baɪk〕n. 摩托車
luckily〔'lʌkɪlɪ〕adv. 幸運地
serious〔'sɪrɪəs〕adj. 嚴重的
settle〔'sɛtḷ〕v. 解決；和解　　**in the end** 最後

fortunately ('fɔrtʃənɪtlɪ) adv. 幸運地
careful ('kɛrfəl) adj. 小心的
experience (ɪk'spɪrɪəns) v. 經歷

7. **Q** : Someone is smoking in a no-smoking area. What can you say to him or her?

   有人正在禁煙區抽煙。你能對他或她說什麼？

A1: I'd say, "Excuse me, but smoking is not allowed here. Maybe you didn't see the sign. You should put it out before you get a fine."

我會說：「對不起，這裡不准抽煙。你可能沒看到告示。你應該在被罰款之前將它熄滅。」

A2: I'd say, "Would you mind putting out your cigarette? The smoke is really bothering me. Besides, you can't smoke here."

我會說：「你介意將你的香煙熄滅嗎？這些煙霧真的很困擾我。此外，你不能在這裡抽煙。」

【註】 smoke (smok) v. 抽煙　n. 煙；煙霧
area ('ɛrɪə) n. 地區　　*no-smoking area* 禁煙區
allow (ə'lau) v. 允許　　maybe ('mebɪ) adv. 或許
sign (saɪn) n. 告示　　*put out* 熄滅
fine (faɪn) n. 罰款　　mind (maɪnd) v. 介意
cigarette ('sɪgə,rɛt) n. 香煙　　bother ('baðɚ) v. 困擾

* 請將下列自我介紹的句子再唸一遍，請開始。

My seat number is (複試座位號碼後 5 碼) , and my test number is (初試准考證號碼後 5 碼) .

初級英語檢定複試測驗 ⑩ 詳解

寫作能力測驗詳解

第一部份：單句寫作

第 1～5 題：句子改寫

1. John swims well.

   John can _____.

   > 重點結構：can 的用法
   >
   > 解　答：John can swim well.
   >
   > 句型分析：主詞＋can＋原形動詞＋副詞
   >
   > 説　明：助動詞 can 後面須接原形動詞，故 swims 須改為 swim。本句的句意為：「約翰可以游得很好。」

2. Joe won't forget to hand in the homework tomorrow.

   Joe _____ yesterday.

   > 重點結構：未來式改為過去式
   >
   > 解　答：Joe didn't forget to hand in the homework yesterday.
   >
   > 句型分析：主詞＋否定助動詞＋原形動詞＋不定詞＋受詞＋時間副詞
   >
   > 説　明：時態由未來式改為過去式，動詞由 won't forget 改為 didn't forget。本句的句意為：「喬昨天並未忘記交家庭作業。」

   > * ***hand in*** 繳交　　homework〔ˋhom͵wɝk〕*n.* 功課；家庭作業

3. My sister was washing the dishes when I got home.

   My sister _____ every day.

   重點結構：過去進行式改爲現在簡單式

   解　答：<u>My sister washes the dishes every day.</u>

   句型分析：主詞＋動詞＋受詞＋時間副詞

   説　明：時態由過去進行式改爲現在簡單式，故 was
   washing 改爲 washes。本句的句意爲：「我的
   姊姊每天洗碗。」

   * dishes〔'dɪʃɪz〕*n. pl.* 待洗的餐具

4. Do you ever go to Joe's Restaurant?

   _____ to Joe's Restaurant yet?

   重點結構：ever 和 yet 的用法

   解　答：<u>Have you gone to Joe's Restaurant yet?</u>

   句型分析：Have＋主詞＋過去分詞＋介系詞＋受詞＋yet？

   説　明：由句尾的副詞 yet（已經）可知，本句爲現在完成
   式，故原句的 Do you ever go to 須改爲 Have
   you gone to。本句的句意爲：「你已經去了喬的
   餐廳了嗎？」

   * ever〔'ɛvɚ〕*adv.* 曾經

5. Where is the dictionary?

   Can you tell me _____?

   重點結構：名詞子句的用法

   解　答：<u>Can you tell me where the dictionary is?</u>

句型分析：助動詞＋主詞＋原形動詞＋受詞＋疑問副詞＋主詞
　　　　　＋be 動詞？

　説　明：tell *sb. sth.*「告訴某人某事」，間接受詞 me 之
　　　　　後，須接直接受詞，故須將疑問句改為名詞子句，
　　　　　即「疑問詞＋主詞＋動詞」的形式，寫成 where
　　　　　the dictionary is。本句的句意為：「你能告訴我
　　　　　那本字典在哪裡嗎？」

　* dictionary〔ˈdɪkʃənˌɛrɪ〕*n.* 字典

第 6～10 題：句子合併

6. We can't get tickets.

　We can't go to the concert.

　If _____.

　重點結構：If 的用法

　　解　答：If we can't get tickets, we can't go to the
　　　　　concert.

　句型分析：If＋主詞＋否定助動詞＋原形動詞＋受詞＋,＋主詞
　　　　　＋否定助動詞＋原形動詞＋介系詞＋受詞

　　説　明：If 引導表條件的副詞子句，修飾主要動詞 go。
　　　　　本句的句意為：「如果我們拿不到票，就無法去
　　　　　演唱會。」

　* concert〔ˈkɑnsɝt〕*n.* 音樂會；演唱會

7. Sally has a coat.

　The coat is made of leather.

　Sally _____ coat.

重點結構：形容詞修飾名詞

解　答：<u>Sally has a leather coat.</u>

句型分析：主詞＋動詞＋不定冠詞＋形容詞＋名詞

說　明：本句的句意為：「莎莉有一件皮製的外套。」
leather 在此為形容詞，作「皮製的」解，放在所
修飾的名詞 coat（外套）前。

＊ leather〔ˈlɛðɚ〕n. 皮革　adj. 皮製的

8. Where are the keys?

I put the keys on the table.

_____ that _____?

重點結構：that 的用法

解　答：<u>Where are the keys that I put on the table?</u>

句型分析：疑問副詞＋be 動詞＋主詞＋that 引導的形容詞
子句？

說　明：that 引導形容詞子句，修飾先行詞 the keys。本句
的句意為：「我放在桌上的那些鑰匙在哪裡？」

9. You can play computer games.

You finish your homework.

You can't _____ until _____.

重點結構：not…until 的用法

解　答：<u>You can't play computer games until you finish</u>
<u>your homework.</u>

句型分析：主詞＋否定助動詞＋原形動詞＋受詞＋until＋主詞
＋動詞＋受詞

　説　明：not…until～表「直到～才…」。本句的句意為：

　　　　　　「直到你做完功課，才能玩電腦遊戲。」

　* finish〔'fɪnɪʃ〕v. 做完　　computer〔kəm'pjutɚ〕n. 電腦

10. We can go to a movie tonight.

　　We can go to a KTV tonight.

　　_____ or _____ tonight.

　重點結構：or 的用法

　　解　答：<u>We can go to a movie or a KTV tonight.</u>

　句型分析：主詞＋助動詞＋原形動詞＋介系詞＋A＋or＋B＋
　　　　　　時間副詞

　　説　明：本句的句意為：「我們今晚可以去看電影或唱
　　　　　　KTV。」

第 11～15 題：重組

11. Why _____?

　　you / the doctor / yesterday / go to / didn't

　重點結構：疑問句的用法

　　解　答：<u>Why didn't you go to the doctor yesterday?</u>

　句型分析：疑問副詞＋否定助動詞＋主詞＋動詞片語＋時間
　　　　　　副詞？

　　説　明：疑問副詞置於句首，主詞和動詞須倒裝，否定助動
　　　　　　詞 didn't 置於主詞 you 之前，再加原形動詞 go to，
　　　　　　再接受詞 the doctor，而 yesterday 置於句尾。

　* ***go to the doctor*** 去看醫生

12. The woman _____.

at the park / to / that / talked / I / my neighbor / is

重點結構：that 的用法

解　答：<u>The woman that I talked to at the park yesterday
is my neighbor.</u>

句型分析：主詞＋that 引導的形容詞子句＋be 動詞＋主詞補語

説　明：關代 that 引導形容詞子句，修飾先行詞 The
woman。本句的句意為：「和我昨天在公園談話的
那個女人是我的鄰居。」

＊ neighbor〔'nebɚ〕n. 鄰居

13. Alice _____.

piano / her / go to / has / class / to

重點結構：has to 的用法

解　答：<u>Alice has to go to her piano class.</u>

句型分析：主詞＋has to＋原形動詞＋介系詞＋受詞

説　明：has to（必須）須接原形動詞。
本句的句意為：「艾莉絲必須去上她的鋼琴課。」

14. Glen _____.

always / Italy / go to / has / to / wanted

重點結構：頻率副詞的用法

解　答：<u>Glen has always wanted to go to Italy.</u>

句型分析：主詞＋has＋頻率副詞＋過去分詞＋不定詞＋介系詞
＋受詞

　　　　　說　明：always（總是）為頻率副詞，須置於一般動詞前，

　　　　　　　　　　be 動詞之後。本句的句意為：「葛倫一直很想去

　　　　　　　　　　義大利。」

　　　　* Italy〔'ɪtl̩ɪ〕 *n.* 義大利

15.　The ＿＿＿＿＿＿＿＿＿＿＿＿＿＿＿＿＿＿＿＿＿.

　　, so / at 9:00 / the station / train / we / should go to / leaves /

　　now

　　　重點結構：so 的用法

　　　　解　答：<u>The train leaves at 9:00, so we should go to the</u>

　　　　　　　　<u>station now.</u>

　　　句型分析：主詞＋動詞＋時間副詞＋,＋so＋主詞＋助動詞＋

　　　　　　　　原形動詞＋介系詞＋受詞＋時間副詞

　　　　說　明：用表「結果」的連接詞 so（所以）連接兩句話。

　　　　　　　　本句的句意為：「火車九點開，所以我們應該現在

　　　　　　　　去車站。」

　　　　* leave〔liv〕 *v.* 離開　　　station〔'steʃən〕 *n.* 車站

第二部份：段落寫作

題目：Mr. Brown 在樂器店門口回想學生時彈吉他的日子。請根據

　　　以下的圖片寫一篇約 50 字的短文。**注意**：未依提示作答者，

　　　將予扣分。

Mr. Brown used to play the guitar when he was a young student, but he had not played music for a long time. ***One day***, he passed by the window of an instrument shop. He looked at the guitars and remembered his student days. The shopkeeper saw Mr. Brown and invited him into the shop to play. Mr. Brown could still play the guitar well, and he had a good time in the shop.

　　以前當布朗先生是個年輕的學生時，他會彈吉他，但是他已經有很長的一段時間沒有玩音樂了。有一天，他經過一家樂器行的櫥窗。他看著那些吉他，想起他的學生時代。老闆看到布朗先生，邀請他進到店裡去演奏。布朗先生吉他仍然彈得很好，所以他在那家店裡玩得很愉快。

used to 以前　　play〔ple〕v. 演奏
guitar〔gɪˋtɑr〕n. 吉他　　***pass by*** 經過
window〔ˋwɪndo〕n. 櫥窗
instrument〔ˋɪnstrəmənt〕n. 工具；樂器（= *musical instrument*）　　***look at*** 看著
remember〔rɪˋmɛmbɚ〕v. 想起
days〔dez〕n. pl. 時代；時期
shopkeeper〔ˋʃɑpˌkipɚ〕n. 店主；老闆
invite〔ɪnˋvaɪt〕v. 邀請　　still〔stɪl〕adv. 仍然
have a good time 玩得愉快

口說能力測驗詳解

* 請在 15 秒內完成並唸出下列自我介紹的句子，請開始。

My seat number is （複試座位號碼後 5 碼）, and my test number is （初試准考證號碼後 5 碼）.

I. 複誦

共五題。題目不印在試卷上，由耳機播出，每題播出兩次，兩次之間大約有一到二秒的間隔。聽完兩次後，請馬上複誦一次。

1. Is Bill or John playing the game?
   正在玩遊戲的是比爾還是約翰？

2. Don't worry. The test is easy.
   不要擔心。這項測驗很容易。

3. How long have you been waiting?
   你等多久了？

4. Make yourselves at home. 不要拘束。

5. Will you take the bus?
   你會搭公車嗎？

【註】 worry〔ˋwɝɪ〕v. 擔心　　*at home* 自在
make yourselves at home 不要拘束（就像在自己家一樣）
take〔tek〕v. 搭乘

II. 朗讀句子與短文

共有五個句子及一篇短文，請先利用一分
鐘的時間閱讀試卷上的句子與短文，然後
在一分鐘內以正常的速度，清楚正確地朗
讀一遍，請開始閱讀。

One : Remember to turn off the lights when you leave the
room. 當你離開房間時，記得要把燈關掉。

Two : What time do you expect to arrive tomorrow?
你預計明天何時會到？

Three : You'd like to go to the amusement park, wouldn't
you? 你想要去遊樂園，不是嗎？

Four : Did you enjoy the exhibition at the museum?
你喜歡博物館的那場展覽嗎？

【註】 ***turn off*** 關掉（電源）　　　light〔laɪt〕*n.* 燈
expect〔ɪkˈspɛkt〕*v.* 預期　　arrive〔əˈraɪv〕*v.* 到達
would like to V. 想要… (= *want to V.*)
amusement〔əˈmjuzmənt〕*n.* 娛樂
amusement park 遊樂場；遊樂園
enjoy〔ɪnˈdʒɔɪ〕*v.* 喜歡
exhibition〔ˌɛksəˈbɪʃən〕*n.* 展覽；展覽會
museum〔mjuˈziəm〕*n.* 博物館

Five　：Please put the ice cream back in the freezer before it melts. 請在冰淇淋融化之前，把它放回冷凍庫。

Six　：Before packing for a trip, there are several things to consider. First of all, what will you be doing during the trip? Will you need formal clothes or casual ones? Also, consider the weather at your destination. Will it be cold or hot? Is it likely to rain? Finally, select clothes that are light and washable.

在為一趟旅行打包之前，有幾件事需要考慮。首先，你會在旅行時做什麼？你會需要正式或休閒的衣服？此外，要考慮目的地的天氣。是寒冷還是炎熱？可能會下雨嗎？最後，選擇輕便而且耐洗的衣服。

【註】 *ice cream* 冰淇淋　　freezer ('frizɚ) *n.* 冷凍庫
melt (mɛlt) *v.* 融化　　pack (pæk) *v.* 打包
trip (trɪp) *n.* 旅行　　consider (kən'sɪdɚ) *v.* 考慮
first of all 首先　　formal ('fɔrml̩) *adj.* 正式的
clothes (kloz) *n. pl.* 衣服　　casual ('kæʒuəl) *adj.* 休閒的
also ('ɔlso) *adv.* 此外　　weather ('wɛðɚ) *n.* 天氣
destination (ˌdɛstə'neʃən) *n.* 目的地
likely ('laɪklɪ) *adj.* 可能的　　finally ('faɪnl̩ɪ) *adv.* 最後
select (sə'lɛkt) *v.* 選擇　　light (laɪt) *adj.* 輕的
washable ('waʃəbl̩) *adj.* 可洗的；耐洗的

III. 回答問題

共七題。題目不印在試卷上，由耳機播出，
每題播出兩次，兩次之間大約有一到二秒的
間隔。聽完兩次後，請馬上回答。每題回答
時間爲 15 秒，請在作答時間內儘量地表達。

1. **Q** : Did you have a long way to come here?
   你來這裡的路途遙遠嗎？

   A1: No, I live pretty close. I could have even walked here.
   But I took a bus, and it took only ten minutes.
   不會，我住得相當近。我原本甚至可以走路來這裡。但我
   搭了公車，只花了十分鐘。

   A2: Yes, I don't live in the city. I took a train early this
   morning. All together, it took me almost two hours to
   get here.
   是的，我不住在城裡。我今天早上很早就搭火車。總共花
   了我幾乎兩小時才到這裡。

   【註】 way〔we〕*n.* 路程；距離　　pretty〔'prɪtɪ〕*adv.* 相當
   close〔klos〕*adv.* 接近地
   could have + ***p.p.*** 原本可以…
   even〔'ivən〕*adv.* 甚至　　early〔'ɝlɪ〕*adv.* 清晨；清早
   all together 總共　　almost〔'ɔl,most〕*adv.* 幾乎

2. **Q** : Are you going to work or school tomorrow?
   你明天要去上班或上學嗎？

   A1: Yes, I am. I work Monday through Friday. I have to
   be in the office at 9:00 tomorrow.

是的，我要去。我星期一至星期五上班。我明天必須九點
到辦公室。

A2: No, I'm not. Tomorrow is a holiday. I'll be happy to
have a day off.

不，我不用。明天是假日。我很高興可以休息一天。

【註】 through〔θru〕*prep.* 從⋯直到
office〔'ɔfɪs〕*n.* 辦公室　　holiday〔'hɑlə,de〕*n.* 假日
off〔ɔf〕*adv.* 休息　　***have a day off*** 休息一天

3. **Q** ： What is your hometown like?
你的家鄉是什麼樣子的？

A1: It's a very small place. There isn't a lot to do there,
but the environment is nice. It's very green and pretty.

它是一個非常小的地方。那裡沒有很多事可做，但環境很
好。一片綠油油，而且很漂亮。

A2: I'm from a pretty big city. It's a busy place with lots
of traffic and big buildings. But there are also some
nice parks.

我來自一座相當大的城市。是個很熱門的地方，它有很多
車輛和大樓。但是也有一些很好的公園。

【註】 hometown〔'hom'taʊn〕*n.* 故鄉；家鄉
environment〔ɪn'vaɪrənmənt〕*n.* 環境
nice〔naɪs〕*adj.* 好的　　green〔grin〕*adj.* 綠油油的
pretty〔'prɪtɪ〕*adv.* 相當　*adj.* 漂亮的
busy〔'bɪzɪ〕*adj.* 繁忙的；熱鬧的　　***lots of*** 很多的
traffic〔'træfɪk〕*n.* 交通；往來的車輛
building〔'bɪldɪŋ〕*n.* 大樓；建築物

4. **Q** : Have you ever thought about having plastic surgery?
Why? 你曾經考慮過整型嗎？爲什麼？

A1: No, never. I think it's unnatural. Besides, it can be
dangerous.

不，從未考慮過。我認爲那不自然。此外，可能會有危險。

A2: Yes, I have. It's becoming more and more common
these days. If I could afford it, I'd do it.

是的，我考慮過。最近整型變得越來越普遍。如果我負擔
得起，我會去整型。

【註】 ***think about*** 考慮
plastic〔'plæstɪk〕*adj.* 塑膠的；整型的
surgery〔's͵dʒərɪ〕*n.* 手術
plastic surgery 整型手術　　never〔'nɛvə〕*adv.* 從未
unnatural〔ʌn'nætʃərəl〕*adj.* 不自然的
besides〔bɪ'saɪdz〕*adv.* 此外
dangerous〔'dendʒərəs〕*adj.* 危險的
more and more 越來越
common〔'kɑmən〕*adj.* 常見的；普通的
these days 最近　　afford〔ə'fɔrd〕*v.* 負擔得起

5. **Q** : When was the last time you used a computer? What
did you use it for?

你上一次用電腦是什麼時候？你爲什麼要用電腦？

A1: I use a computer every day. In fact, I used one this
morning. I checked the news and my e-mail.

我每天都會使用電腦。事實上，我今天早上就有使用。我
查看新聞和我的電子郵件。

A2: I haven't used a computer since Tuesday. I was
looking for some information on the Internet. I found
what I needed easily.

我從星期二以來就沒用過電腦。我當時是在網路上找一些
資訊。我很輕易地就找到我需要的資訊。

【註】 *last time* 上一次
　　　 What…for? 為什麼…？ (= *Why…?*)
　　　 in fact 事實上　　　check〔 tʃɛk 〕*v.* 查看
　　　 news〔 njuz 〕*n.* 新聞　　e-mail〔'i,mel 〕*n.* 電子郵件
　　　 look for 尋找　　　information〔,ɪnfɚ'meʃən 〕*n.* 資訊
　　　 Internet〔'ɪntɚ,nɛt 〕*n.* 網際網路
　　　 easily〔'izɪlɪ 〕*adv.* 輕易地

6. **Q**　: Have you ever stayed in the hospital?
　　　 你曾經住過院嗎？

A1: No, I've never had to stay there overnight. I'm a
pretty healthy person. In fact, I rarely even go to the
doctor.

不，我從不需要在那裡過夜。我相當健康。事實上，我甚
至很少去看醫生。

A2: Yes, I had an operation when I was a child. I had to
have my tonsils taken out. I was very young, so I
don't remember it very well.

是的，我小時候動過手術。我必須摘除扁桃腺。我當時年
紀很小，所以記得不是很清楚。

【註】 stay〔 ste 〕*v.* 停留；暫住　　*stay in the hospital* 住院
　　　 overnight〔'ovɚ'naɪt 〕*adv.* 整夜

healthy〔ˈhɛlθɪ〕 *adj.* 健康的　　rarely〔ˈrɛrlɪ〕 *adv.* 很少
operation〔͵ɑpəˈreʃən〕 *n.* 手術
tonsil〔ˈtɑnsḷ〕 *n.* 扁桃腺　　*take out* 除去
remember it very well 記得很清楚

7. **Q**：Your friend did poorly in a talent contest. What can
　　you say to him or her?

　　你的朋友在才藝比賽中表現得不好。你能對他或她說什麼？

A1: I'd say, "Cheer up. You were better than you think.
　　The important thing is that you tried."

　　我會說：「要振作起來。你比你所想的要好。重要的是，
　　你盡力了。」

A2: I'd say, "Don't worry. You'll do better next time.
　　You just need a little more practice."

　　我會說：「別擔心。你下次會表現得更好。你只是需要多
　　一點練習。」

【註】 do〔du〕 *v.* 表現　　poorly〔ˈpʊrlɪ〕 *adv.* 差勁地
　　talent〔ˈtælənt〕 *n.* 才能
　　contest〔ˈkɑntɛst〕 *n.* 比賽　　***cheer up*** 振作起來
　　important〔ɪmˈpɔrtṇt〕 *adj.* 重要的
　　try〔traɪ〕 *v.* 嘗試；努力　　***next time*** 下一次
　　practice〔ˈpræktɪs〕 *n.* 練習

＊請將下列自我介紹的句子再唸一遍，請開始。

My seat number is （複試座位號碼後 5 碼）, and my test
number is （初試准考證號碼後 5 碼）.